Beyond Happily Ever After

CHOOSE YOUR OWN FAIRY TALE ENDING

TERI LOTT

For all the lovers of stories – the listeners, the readers, and the tellers. And especially for all of the fairy tale lovers, like me, who enjoy hearing these stories over and over again.

I'm grateful to everyone who has continued to encourage me to keep sharing my stories.

Special thanks to A.L. Hatcher, a phenomenal author and friend without whom this book would not have been published.

Contents

Part One

Stories of Talking Animals, Magical Creatures, and the Like

The Gingerbread Man

I know what you are thinking. How can there be more to the story of the Gingerbread Man? Well, as a matter of fact there is.

You probably know how the Gingerbread Man came to be in existence. He was created by a little old woman who wanted a little boy. But as soon as he came out of the oven, cooled down and was decorated, he jumped off the cookie sheet and ran away from the little old woman and little old man. He also ran away from the cat, the dog, the cow, the sheep, and the horse. Then he came to a river.

He couldn't cross it on his own. Just like Santa's cookies dissolve in the milk you leave him, a Gingerbread Man would melt in the freshwater of a river. So, he accepted a ride from a fox who just happened to be sunning himself on the riverbank. Despite his initial misgivings, the Gingerbread Man jumped on his back near the fox's tail. But the water got deeper, so he jumped up onto the fox's back near his shoulders. But the water got even deeper, so he jumped onto the fox's head. That's when the fox twisted his head around and ate the Gingerbread Man.

At least that's how the traditional ending goes. But think about it. The Gingerbread Man was a pretty clever cookie, would he really allow the fox to eat him?

Let me tell you what really happened. As the fox twisted his head around, the Gingerbread Man also twisted so the fox only bit off the Gingerbread Man's left leg. By now they were close to the riverbank, so the Gingerbread Man hopped onto the bank and kept hopping as fast as he could go. The fox was so startled, he didn't even follow the Gingerbread Man.

It didn't take long for the Gingerbread Man to be completely exhausted. After all, he had been running around all day and had just experienced a traumatic event. He found a small cave and laid down. He was asleep within moments, only to be awakened a brief time later when he heard a low growl. It was a bear cub. She had also been asleep, but the smell of the Gingerbread Man had awakened her. Before the Gingerbread Man knew it, she had bitten off his left arm. She might have eaten more, but the

Gingerbread Man jumped up and hopped out of the cave as fast as his right leg would take him.

He came across a footbridge and hopped across it. Once he was on the other side of the river, he looked for someplace safe to sleep. He found a tree whose trunk had a hollowed-out place. He hopped into the empty space and laid down. Again, he was snoozing within seconds. He was sleeping so soundly, he didn't even feel the porcupine, whose home he had stumbled across, nibbling on his right hand. When the porcupine got to his wrist, he woke up, jumped up, and began hopping away. The porcupine was too tired to follow and simply laid down and went back to sleep with visions of gingerbread dancing in his head.

The Gingerbread Man kept hopping and hopping, weary and completely disoriented now. He saw a barn up ahead and thought he might be able to hide under some hay and finally get some sleep. And that's what he did. This time he slept through the night but was awakened early in the morning by something nibbling on his right arm. It was a mouse who lived in the barn and had gone into the hay to catch forty winks. The Gingerbread Man shook his arm, and the mouse flew off. She wasn't badly hurt but was stunned enough not to give chase.

Now you have a choice, a pleasant ending for The Gingerbread Man or a just desserts ending.

Pleasant Ending

The Gingerbread Man was off and hopping again. But in the early morning light he realized where he was. He had slept in the barn of the little old woman and the little old man! And at that moment, the old man had stepped out onto the porch to smoke his pipe. He saw the Gingerbread Man and a big wide grin lit up his face. "Welcome home, son! Looks like you've had a spot of trouble. Why don't you come into the house? I bet the missus can fix you right up."

And that's how the little old woman and the little old man finally got a son. And do you know what? They did all live happily ever after.

Just Desserts Ending

The Gingerbread Man was off and hopping again. But in the early morning light he realized where he was. He had slept in the barn of the little old woman and the little old man! And at that moment, the old man had stepped out onto the porch to smoke his pipe. He saw the Gingerbread Man and a big wide grin lit up his face.

"Well, there you are! You gave us quite the chase little fella. Come on in the house, the missus is getting breakfast ready. She'll be happy to see you."

And so the Gingerbread Man hopped into the kitchen. A big smile filled the old woman's face when she saw him. "Well, now, you've come home, have ya? I think we can break the rules this once, can't we Pa?"

"Sure, we can," was his reply. "After all, we're not getting any younger so why not eat dessert first?"

"Crunch, crunch, crunch." And that was the end of the Gingerbread Man. And do you know what? He was mighty tasty! "Yum, yum, yummy!"

The Three Little Pigs

You probably heard the story of the three little pigs when you were a youngster. Mama Pig sent her three sons out into the world to make their own way. The first little pig was rather lazy and built his house out of the first thing he could find – straw. The big bad wolf comes along and blows the pig's house down, but the pig is able to escape by the hair of his chinny chin chin and races to his brother's house. Now this brother wasn't much brighter. He built his house out of sticks. And history repeats itself. The two brothers make it to the third brother's house. Now he was a precocious porker. He built his house out of bricks which withstand the huffing and puffing of the big, bad wolf. But the wolf is tenacious and tries going down the chimney. Unfortunately for the wolf, the third brother has that covered and has a big pot of boiling water in his fireplace. So the wolf does not get his ham dinner and instead loses his life.

Well those three brothers should have lived happily ever after except they didn't. You see, the first two little pigs were sloppy sluggards. They ate like, well like pigs, so food fell from their mouths as they chomped and chewed. And they didn't restrict their eating to the kitchen. They ate all over the house so there were chunks of food and dirty dishes everywhere.

And that wasn't the end of their slovenliness, oh no. Their dirty, stinky clothes were strewn all over the floor of their bedrooms. Their clothes were stinky because they didn't bathe too often. When they finally did bathe a grimy, gray ring was left in the bathtub. The bathroom was always a mess with squirts of toothpaste in the sink, wet towels on the floor, and hair from their chinny chin chins everywhere.

Both of the pigs had sinus issues, so they went through a lot of tissues. But neither of them seemed to think trash cans were useful household items, so those snotty tissues ended up everywhere too. It didn't take more than a week of this before the third little pig, who was a neat freak, told them they'd have to build their own houses.

Now even though they were slobs, they had learned something from their experiences with the big bad wolf. They were not going to use the inferior materials of straw or sticks this time, oh no. They were going to build brick houses of their own.

There was a big problem with their plan, however. You see they didn't have the expertise to build a brick house correctly and they weren't going to ask their brother since the "insensitive jerk" was throwing them out.

So the first brother stacked his bricks in a grapevine pattern, using no mortar between the bricks. The day he moved in, the big bad wolf's brother drops by. All he had to do was huff and puff one time and that house fell apart. Before you can say, "not by the hair of my chinny, chin, chin" the wolf ate the first little pig. Not only did it taste delicious, but it also completed step one in the wolf's plan to avenge his brother.

The other brother was a bit brighter. He knew to use mortar between the bricks. He mixed his mortar but didn't use the correct proportions of cement and sand. The day he moved in, the big bad wolf's brother pays a call. He huffs and puffs and huffs and puffs and the house is blown down. And before you can say, "not by the hair of my chinny, chin, chin" the second little pig finds himself the wolf's next meal. Step two of the wolf's plan is complete.

Pleasant Ending

Now the wolf was aware of what happened to his brother at the third little pig's house, and he knew that this pig had a well-built house and was very clever, so he decided he was satisfied with two ham dinners and left.

And the third little pig? Well after he finished cleaning and sanitizing his house he lived a long, long life. And although he did miss his less than clever brothers, I guess you could say he lived happily ever after.

Just Desserts Ending

The third little pig was incensed about what happened to his two brothers and he wanted revenge. So after a memorial service for his brothers – they couldn't really have a burial, after all – he devised a very clever plan.

You may not be aware of this, but the third little pig was quite the seamstress. He had learned everything he knew from watching YouTube videos. He created a stuffed pig that was so realistic, it could have been his brother. He stuffed the pig with aromatic packets that were bacon scented.

This new little pig was placed on top of an old well that had been in danger of collapsing for years. To make the bacon aroma more prevalent, the third little pig cooked bacon each morning with his kitchen window open. After a few days, the scent of the bacon caught the attention of the big bad wolf's brother's acute sniffer, and he followed the smell to the fourth little pig.

As soon as the wolf saw the pig, he quickly surveyed the area, and seeing no one around, pounced on him. The force of that pounce caused the old, rotten wood that was covering the well to give way and the wolf descended at a rapid rate, still holding the fourth little pig. Although the little pig was quite padded, it did nothing to protect the wolf and he met his death when he landed at the bottom of that old, moldy, dry well.

The third little pig got his revenge and spent the rest of his days trying to live life to the fullest. After all, you never know when you might meet up with a big, bad wolf.

Jack and the Beanstalk

One of my favorite story characters is Jack. In fact, I've written several of my own Jack tales. The original story of *Jack and the Beanstalk* is more than 250 years old.

Jack lives with his widowed mother and they are extremely poor. Jack is sent to market to sell the only thing they have left of any value, their cow Milky White. Along the way Jack meets an old man who trades him five magic beans for the cow. When Jack returns home, his mother is so angry she throws them out the window.

The next day there is a beanstalk going up into the sky. Jack climbs it and finds himself in a magical place in the clouds.

He first meets the giant's wife who is kind to Jack but then the giant comes home. He has a super sensitive nose and says, "Fee fi fo fum, I smell the blood of an Englishman." His wife is able to convince him that he is smelling the last person he ate.

Jack makes several trips up and down the beanstalk, taking a bag of gold, a goose who lays golden eggs, and a magic golden harp. But as Jack is carrying the harp away, she alerts the giant who begins to chase Jack. Jack is able to descend the beanstalk and chop it down with an axe. The story ends with Jack and his mother being set for life.

But I ask you to consider - Do zebras change their stripes? Well Jack certainly didn't change overnight. He developed gold fever and went crazy spending the gold. He bought new clothes and shoes for himself, a new feather filled mattress, sports equipment, and lots and lots of candy – Jack had quite the sweet tooth. He also bought new pots and pans for his mom – the better for her to cook with – and chickens, geese, piglets, and a new cow.

Before you could say, "Jack and the Beanstalk," all the gold was gone. Jack's mother was very upset with him. You can believe that his ears were boxed several times!

Luckily, they still had the goose who laid golden eggs. Knowing she couldn't trust Jack's judgement; Jack's mother collected the eggs very early in the morning before Jack got up and hid them in the house until she could get to town and exchange them for food or whatever they needed.

Now as we know, Jack was not the sharpest crayon in the box and one day when his mother was in town, he thought he'd help her out and kill and de-feather one of their geese for dinner. He knew exactly what to do, if he looked under a goose and there were no golden eggs then it would be safe to kill that one. And so the deed is done.

Jack's mother returned home just as Jack completed plucking the goose. Her face lost all color as she asked Jack, "How did you know which goose to kill?" As Jack explained, her face turned as red as beet. "Jack, I had already removed the eggs. You killed our golden goose!"

Pleasant Ending

Well, what could Jack's mother do? We love our children no matter what. And they did still have the golden harp and the farm animals Jack had bought. They'd get by.

After all, Jack's mother was used to economizing and getting by on next to nothing. She just needed to make sure that Jack did not have access to the golden harp. So what did she do? I'm so glad you asked. She hid the harp in a place where Jack never went – the utility closet where the broom, dustpan, mop, and bucket were kept!

And so they were able to live happily ever after, or at least as happy as a mother with a son like Jack could live.

Just Desserts Ending

Well, no amount of ear boxing was going to fix this, or for that matter fix Jack. Jack's mother realized he was never going to develop any common sense living under her roof, so the solution was simple - she kicked Jack out. Now I know this may seem harsh, but he was in his early twenties after all and besides, the poor woman was at her wits end! And she didn't send him out in the world without anything. He left with a bundle that contained a couple of changes of clothes, several pairs of clean underwear (because moms always make sure we have that) and enough food to last him for a week or more.

Jack had many adventures after that, but those are stories for another time. And his mother? Well she had always lived a simple life and with the farm animals and selling the singing golden harp she had enough money to support herself for the rest of her days. And those days were more peaceful without Jack around.

Goldilocks and The Three Bears

Ah, Goldilocks. The little girl who wanders into the home of the three bears when they have gone off for a morning walk. She tries each bowl of their porridge and finds one too hot (Papa Bear's), one too cold (Mama Bear's) and one just right (Baby Bear's) She eats all of the porridge in the last bowl.

Feeling a bit tired, and also being nosy, she makes her way into the sitting room and tries the three chairs. Papa Bear's is too hard, Mama Bear's is too soft, but Baby Bear's is just right. Baby Bear's chair is a rocking chair and Goldilocks rocks so hard she breaks it!

Still feeling tired she makes her way to the bedroom. The biggest bed is too hard, the next bed is too soft – in fact, she almost smothers in the pillows and mattress – but the third bed is just right, and she falls into a deep sleep.

The Bear family comes home from their walk and discovers the porridge and chair situations and then they go into their bedroom. Baby Bear finds Goldilocks asleep in his bed. He calls out to his parents who rush over to join him. Goldilocks opens her eyes, screams, and runs out of the house. But that's not the end of the story.

Pleasant Ending

Goldilocks gets home and her parents ask where she has been. She shares the entire story. They are so appalled by her behavior that they tell her they are all going to the Bear family's house the next day for her to apologize. Goldie's mom, Mrs. Golden, makes a delicious breakfast casserole and her dad makes his famous blueberry muffins. They also take some tools with them. The three walk to the bears' home. Goldie skips a bit ahead of her parents.

The bears are just heading out for their morning constitutional. Baby Bear sees Goldilocks and cries out, "There she is again, the girl who ate all my porridge and broke my chair!"

Mama Bear says, "Oh my. I'm surprised she is showing her face again." Papa Bear just growls. The color drains from Goldilocks' face just as her parents come into view.

"Hello," her mom calls out.

"Goldie," her dad says, "Have you apologized yet?" At this, Papa Bear stops growling, and the three bears look at Goldilocks.

"I'm very sorry for coming into your house without being invited," Goldilocks says very sincerely. "I'll never do it again," she adds.

Her mom steps up and holds out the breakfast casserole, "Hi, I'm Mrs. Golden, Goldie's mom. We don't know what got into our girl. We have raised her to be more polite. We hope you'll accept our apology as well. I made a breakfast casserole that I hope you'll like."

Mama Bear smiles and takes the casserole. "It smells wonderful. Is that a crunchy honey topping?"

"Yes," Goldie's mom responds. "I thought you'd like that."

At this, Goldie's dad hands Papa Bear the basket of still warm muffins. "I hope you like blueberry muffins."

"Yum," Baby Bear says.

"Oh, I also brought my tools so we can fix that broken chair," Mr. Golden added.

"Why don't we eat this now while everything is still warm? We can take our walk later," says Mama Bear. "Won't you join us for breakfast?" And that is how The Bear family and The Golden family became the best of friends.

Just Desserts Ending

Now brown bears are omnivores, meaning they eat plants and animals. They typically only eat small mammals such as mice or squirrels, but there are three of them and only one little girl. And, after all, they are ravenous from taking their morning constitutional and finding no breakfast waiting for them upon their return. On top of that, they are also angry because Goldilocks broke Baby Bear's chair AND invaded the sanctity of their home.

Needless to say, the three bears give chase, and although Goldilocks has just had a restorative nap, she is no match for the bears. I won't go into the grizzly details, just suffice it to say, the three bears did get a tender, tasty breakfast that morning that was much more filling than bowls of porridge.

Little Red Riding Hood

A child's love for their grandmother – there's nothing like it, is there? Well Little Red Riding Hood certainly loved her grandmother. When she hears she is sick, she asks her mother if she can take a basket of goodies to her. In some stories, its cake, and a little pot of butter in others its cake and a bottle of wine and yet in others its cookies. But whatever it is, Red Riding Hood starts out. She meets a sly wolf along the way who cons the naïve little girl into sharing the location of her grandmother's house and plants the seed that picking her some flowers would be a nice touch.

As Little Red picks said flowers, the wolf races to grandma's house, gains access to the house, eats grandma, puts on her clothes, and slips into her bed. When Little Red arrives and enters she does notice that grandma looks different. She comments, "Oh Granny, what big ears you have."

The wolf responds, "All the better to hear you with."

Next Red says, "Oh, Granny, what big eyes you have."

The wolf replies, "All the better to see you with."

"Oh, Granny," Red continues, "What big teeth you have!"

To which the wolf says, "All the better to eat you with," and commences to eat Little Red Riding Hood – cape and all.

Well that would have been the end of the story except a huntsman who happens by quickly sizes up the situation, kills the wolf and opens him up. Out come Little Red and Grandmother relatively unharmed.

Sounds like a happy ending, right? Well, when the huntsman rescues Little Red and her grandmother by cutting open the wolf's belly, and pulling them out, you can imagine the mess that was on the floor as well as how gooey and goopy Little Red and grandma must have been. So Little Red helps her grandma clean the floor, strip the bed, and put on new bedding. Then they clean themselves up.

But wait, wasn't grandma sick and in bed before the whole wolf incident? Well, grandma is feeling a lot better

– isn't it amazing how your perspective changes about the severity of your illness after being eaten by a wolf?

Pleasant Ending

In fact, grandma is feeling so good that she fixes the huntsmen and Little Red a delicious dinner of roasted turkey with all the fixins'. They enjoy the food and the company, eating until they are quite full.

After helping clean up the kitchen, Little Red gives her grandma a hug and promises to visit again soon. And the huntsman? Well he offers to walk Little Red home to make sure she is safe. Grandma wholeheartedly agrees to the arrangement and bids them goodbye with a sly smile on her face.

Why was grandma smiling? Well, it turns out Little Red's mother is a widow and quite good looking. I'll leave the rest of the story to your imagination.

Just Desserts Ending

The smell of the roasted turkey meal drifts up the chimney and reaches the nose of a slumbering bear. The scent causes the bear's nose to twitch, and it wakes him up. With some difficulty he pulls himself up to his feet not only due to his bulk, but also because he had been in a deep sleep. Following his super sniffer, he makes his way to grandma's house. By this time, Little Red, grandma, and the huntsman have eaten until they are satiated so, of course, their bellies are quite full. The tryptophan in the turkey has made all three quite drowsy. Grandma lays down on her bed, Little Red has put her head on the table and the huntsman, being used to roughin' it, has laid down on the floor. Before the bear arrives, they are all sawing logs.

Bear easily finds the house, guided by the delectable smells coming from the open windows and chimney. Looking forward to a meal of turkey, he climbs through one of the open windows and is greeted by the sight of three sleeping entrees – of which one is snoring, but I'm not going to tell you which one. That, of course, did not deter the hungry bear. You can probably imagine what happened next so I'm not going to spell it out for you. If you're not sure, give it some thought. Thus ends this version of the story of *Little Red Riding Hood*.

Three Billy Goats Gruff

This is one of my favorite tales to tell! The three billy goats gruff are looking for greener grass and locate it across a bridge. Unfortunately, the bridge is controlled by a huge, ugly troll who loves nothing better than devouring goats. So the three brothers develop a plan. The smallest billy goat crosses the bridge – trip, trop, trip, trop – and the troll jumps up from under the bridge and expresses his intention to eat him. The smallest goat convinces the troll to wait until the next brother comes, who is much bigger. So the next brother begins to cross and recent history repeats itself. Finally, the third, biggest brother crosses the bridge. The troll approaches, but the goat butts him with his huge horns. The troll is shoved off the bridge and is carried downstream. The third brother crosses and joins his two brothers. The three billy goats gruff have acres and acres of green grass to eat.

With apologies to Peter Christen Asbjornsen and Jorgen Moe, the Norwegian authors who collected the original *Three Billy Goats Gruff* story, I don't think goats would risk their lives for fields of grass. Although goats do eat grass, it's not their major food source. They actually prefer weeds, ferns and even tree bark. So the lovely hills of tall, tall grass that they found on the other side of the troll's bridge wasn't going to satisfy them for very long.

After a few days, the three brothers went trotting off to look for a great weedy location. It didn't take long before they found what they were looking for! A few miles away was another bridge going over the same stream they had crossed before. But this was an ancient, abandoned, covered bridge. On both sides of the bridge the ground was covered with weeds. And the bridge itself was covered with long, stringy vines. To make things even better, there were trees growing all around and plenty of long, green grass. An area of dense shrubs would also provide them with a place to sleep. It was a billy goat's paradise!

So the brothers settled in. They were very happy with their new location. The first night, when they were snoozing, a strange sound woke up the smallest brother. At first he thought he had been dreaming, but then he heard it again. It sounded like snorting and snoring all at the same time.

He moved his head slightly to the right and lightly butted horns with his brother.

"Hmm, what?" his brother asked sleepily.

"Shhh, listen," said his little brother. They both heard the snorting, snoring sound. The middle brother moved his head slightly to the right and lightly butted horns with the biggest brother.

"Hey, watch it," he said.

"Shhh," said both of the other brothers.

"Listen." And there was the sound again.

"What in the world is that?" the biggest brother said.

"I have no idea," said the middle brother.

"I don't know," said the littlest brother, "but I don't like the sound of it."

"Well, we aren't going to find out by staying here," said the biggest brother. "I'll go check it out."

"Ok," said the middle brother.

"Be careful," said the littlest brother.

The biggest billy goat gruff got to his feet and tried to tiptoe toward the sound – not the easiest thing for a hoofed animal to do. The sound was coming from the old covered bridge and as the goat got closer, the sound seemed to increase in volume tenfold.

Imagine his surprise when he saw what the sound was coming from. For inside the covered bridge was a sleeping ... dragon! And this was no ordinary dragon – if you can call any dragon ordinary – it was a three-headed dragon. The billy goat froze in place for what seemed like hours but was actually only a few seconds before he turned and ran back to his brothers.

His brothers heard him coming. They jumped up ready to flee if necessary.

"You'll never believe what is making that snorting, snoring sound!" he exclaimed in a shaky voice.

"What?" asked the middle brother.

"What?" asked the little brother.

"It's... it's... it's..."

"What??" both brothers cried out.

The biggest brother gulped and said, "A dragon!"

"You're kidding," said the middle brother, "I thought dragons were extinct!"

"I did too," replied the older brother. "But he is inside the covered bridge – and he has not one, not two, but three heads!"

"No, say it isn't so," said the little brother. "Not a dragon with three heads! What are we going to do?"

"I don't know. I don't know. I need time to think," responded the biggest brother.

"Could we try to trick him like we did the troll?" asked the middle brother.

"No," was the reply. "This creature is much bigger than the troll and might be smarter than the troll too."

"What we need is some intel," said the biggest brother.

"Intel?" asked the middle brother. "What is intel?"

"He means information about the dragon," interjected the little brother. Both brothers looked at him, astonishment all over their faces.

"What?" said the little brother. "I know things. Well, some things."

"Great!" said the biggest brother with a bit of sarcasm in his voice. "Do you know how we can get rid of this dragon?"

"Not yet," said the little brother, "but since I'm the smallest I think I should be the one to gather the intel. I can hide in dense shrubs near the bridge." Since neither of the other brothers had a better idea that became the first step of their action plan.

To say that the little brother was delighted would be an understatement. You see, he had not been thrilled about being used as the first decoy in the plot to defeat the troll, nor had he been asked for his input or opinion. This was his chance for redemption. He was going to solve this new problem on his own!

He got up on the ends of his hooves and did his best to tiptoe to the grouping of bushes closest to the covered bridge. He settled down in those bushes and watched the sleeping, snorting, snoring dragon. Right away he noticed that one of the heads had a snarl on its face and that was the head that was snorting. Another head had no expression at all. This was the head that was snoring. And the third head? Well it was emitting no noise, and it was wearing a great big smile.

That would be the one to approach, he decided, but it was probably not the best idea to wake up a sleeping dragon. What was that expression? "Let sleeping dogs lie." The billy goat felt the same would be true about a sleeping dragon. So he decided to wait until morning to talk to the smiling head. But it had been a long day, and before you could say, "Billy Goats Gruff", he was sawing his own logs.

He was awakened the next morning with his brain alerting him to the smell of something burnt filling his nostrils. "The dragon!" he thought and jumped up, only to find himself face to face with the three-headed creature.

He gulped. "Good morning," he said with a squeak.

"Humph," replied the snarling face.

"Good morning," said the smiling face. And the expressionless face said – you guessed it – nothing.

"What are you doing in the bushes?" asked the snarling face.

"Umm... sleeping?" was the billy goat's reply.

"Are you asking us or telling us?" asked the snarling face.

"Umm.. telling you. I was sleeping."

"Do you usually sleep in bushes?" inquired the smiling face.

"Y-y-yes. That's our preferred place to sleep," the billy goat answered.

"Our?" said the snarling face, looking around. "There are more of you?"

Before he could think of what to say, the smiling face said, "You know we saw three of them cross the bridge, so why are you asking him?"

"You, you, saw us?" asked the billy goat.

"Of course we did, dear. We don't miss much with three pair of eyes after all."

"Enough of all of this," the previously silent head said. "I'm hungry, let's eat." The littlest billy goat closed his eyes, certain that he was going to be their breakfast. He thought of his brothers and hoped they would not meet with the same fate.

Pleasant Ending

Then he heard loud munching. He opened his eyes and saw the three heads eating the long, green grass all around him. It turns out that the dragon – all three heads of him – were vegetarians!

Just Desserts Ending

Well, the littlest billy goat shouldn't have had such grandiose ideas, thinking he could gather intel and solve the problem of a three-headed dragon – at least not on his own. He quickly became the first course of what would become a three-course breakfast for the three headed dragon. And how perfect that there was a goat for each head! "Yum, yum, yum."

And thus ends the story of *The Three Billy Goats Gruff*. But don't feel too bad for the goats. They had had a good life and after all, a dragon's got to eat too, right?

Rumpelstiltskin

O nce there was a hardworking miller who didn't have much to his name except his beautiful daughter. One day the King, who had been hunting, stopped by his mill in order to rest and water his horse. Wanting to impress the King, the miller bragged that his daughter could spin straw into gold.

This sounded impossible to the King, and he told the miller just that. The miller kept insisting that his daughter had such a talent. Well, the King wanted to see this amazing feat for himself, so he asked the miller to bring his daughter to the castle. Once she arrived, the King locked her up in a tower room filled with straw and a spinning wheel and demanded she spin the straw into gold by morning or he would have her killed.

The miller's daughter could do nothing but stare at the straw and the spinning wheel. She had never been so miserable! When she had just about given up all hope, a little imp-like man appeared in the room and asked her what she will give him if he spins the straw into gold. She offers him the necklace of glass beads she is wearing around her neck. The little man accepted and in no time at all, the straw has been spun into gold.

The next morning the King opened the door, nodded his head in approval and then took the girl to a larger room filled with straw to repeat the feat. Once again, she spends a terrifying evening, but the imp returns. She offers the glass ring she is wearing for payment. Once again the straw is spun into gold and the little man leaves.

On the next day the girl is taken to an even larger room filled with straw, and told by the King that if she can spin all this straw into gold he will marry her, but if she cannot she will be executed. While she is sobbing alone in the room, the little imp appears again and once again promises that he can spin the straw into gold for her, but the girl tells him she has nothing left with which to pay. The strange creature suggests she pay him with her firstborn child. She reluctantly agrees, and he sets about spinning the straw into gold.

The King keeps his promise to marry the miller's daughter. And just over a year later, their first child is born. When the child is only one day old, the imp returns to claim his payment. She offers him all the wealth she has to keep the child, but the little man has no interest in her riches. He finally agrees to give up his claim to the child if she can guess his name within three days.

The Queen's many guesses fail. On the second night, desperate to keep the child she loves dearly, she wanders into the woods searching for him. She comes across his remote mountain cottage and watches, unseen, as he hops about his fire and sings. He reveals his name in his song's lyrics: "Tonight tonight, my plans I make, tomorrow tomorrow, the baby I take. The Queen will never win the game, for Rumpelstiltskin is my name".

When the imp comes to the Queen on the third day, she makes several intentionally wrong guesses. The strange little man grins at each wrong guess. But then the Queen reveals his name, Rumpelstiltskin, and he loses his temper at the loss of their bargain. In his anger, he drives his right foot down into the ground. The force is so great, so powerful, that he creates a chasm and falls into it.

Now here's the thing, if Rumpelstiltskin has the ability to spin straw into gold, do you think he would be defeated by falling into a chasm? I doubt it very much. So here's what I think really happened.

Rumpelstiltskin tunnels his way out of the chasm and goes back to his mountain cottage to devise his plot to seek revenge. He doesn't act immediately as he wants to lull the Queen into a sense of safety and security.

Since he is small in stature, Rumpelstiltskin is easily able to hide and keep an eye on the happenings in and around the castle. He watches as the young child, a boy named James, grows from infant to toddler. Rumpelstiltskin begins to bring a small ball with him.

While the nursemaid, Martha Jane, dozes in a chair outside on the lawn, Rumpelstiltskin begins to throw the ball to James while keeping himself hidden in the bushes. James comes closer and closer to the bushes until Rumpelstiltskin is able to coax the boy into the brush.

Pleasant Ending

At that very moment, Martha Jane awakens, and after blinking the bright sun out of her eyes, notices that James is missing. She jumps up and screams his name. That alerts the guard who is nearby as well as the Queen who is picking flowers in the garden.

They join the nursemaid in the search for James and find him in another part of the yard with a small red ball in his hand. The Queen grabs James and gives him a crushing hug.

Later, when the Queen is explaining to James that he can't wander off from his nanny, she asks him about the red ball. You see, James has many different sizes and colors of balls – but none of them are red. James replies in a sing-songy voice, "Little man, little man, little man."

Terror grips the Queen's heart as she realizes that Rumpelstiltskin is back in their lives. She had long since confessed to the King about what had taken place with the straw into gold scheme. After all, she didn't want to be put on the spot and asked to do that again, and he had long since forgiven her for that deception. So now she goes to the King and tells him what has happened in the yard.

The King summons all his horses and all his men, and they ride off to find the "little man." I'm not sure if they find him, but I do know that wily Rumpelstiltskin is never seen again.

Just Desserts Ending

The King summons all his horses and all his men. Following directions from the Queen, they first ride to Rumpelstiltskin's mountain cottage. There they find evidence that he has vacated his home.

So the search continues over hill and over dale. Months and months go by. The Queen, at home with their son, is wondering when she'll see her beloved husband again. She is also worried about him and his men; hoping they are safe and not in harm's way.

Meanwhile, the King and his men are becoming discouraged. The King tells them that they will search one more day and then return to the castle. And, as fate would have it, that very next day at dusk they see a wisp of smoke in the sky and following it, they discover a miniature opening in a cave. Inside the cave is a snoozing "little man".

Rumpelstiltskin is grabbed by several of the King's men and tied to a tree. Several other men gather dry twigs and small tree branches to form a ring around the tree. And the King himself started the fire.

They watched as the flames grew and grew. They watched to make sure that the imp did not find a way to break free. They watched to make sure that was the end of Rumpelstiltskin. And it was.

"Tonight tonight, no more plans he'll make, tomorrow tomorrow, the child forever stays safe. The Queen and King won the game, and never again will they hear that Rumpelstiltskin is his name".

Hansel and Gretel

Near a great forest there lived a poor woodcutter, his second wife, and his two children. The boy's name was Hansel and the girl's Gretel. They had very little to eat and times were hard. The woodcutter lay in bed one night tossing and turning. He sighed heavily, and said to his wife, "What will become of us? We cannot even feed our children."

His wife's response was quick; as if she had been planning this for several days. "Early in the morning we will take the children deep into the forest. We will make them a fire, and we will give each of them a piece of bread. Then we will go to another part of the forest to gather wood and leave them alone. They will never find the way home again, and we shall be rid of them."

"No," said the woodcutter, "I cannot do that; I cannot find in my heart to take my children into the forest and to leave them there alone. The wild animals would soon come and devour them."

"You are a fool," she said. "All of us will starve. You had better get the coffins ready."

She constantly nagged him until he consented. The two children had not been able to sleep because they were so hungry and had heard what their stepmother had said to their father. Gretel cried but Hans told her to be quiet, he would think of something.

When their parents had gone to sleep he got up, put on his coat, opened the back door, and slipped out. The moon was shining brightly, and the white stones that lay in front of the house glistened like pieces of silver. Hansel stooped and filled the little pocket of his coat. Then he went back again, and said to Gretel, "Go to sleep now. I have a plan."

Before the sun had risen, the wife came and awakened the two children, saying, "Get up, you lazy bones; we are going into the forest to cut wood." Then she gave each of them a piece of bread, and said, "That is for dinner, and you must not eat it before then for you will get no more."

As they walked through the forest, Hansel kept dropping stones, one at a time, along their path. When they reached the middle of the forest their father told the children to collect wood to make a fire to keep them warm. Hansel and Gretel gathered brushwood and it was set on fire, and when the flame was burning quite high the wife said, "Now lie down by the fire and rest yourselves and we will go and cut wood; and when we are ready we will come and fetch you."

So Hansel and Gretel sat by the fire, and at noon they each ate their pieces of bread. They thought their father was in the wood all the time, as they seemed to hear the strokes of the axe; but really it was only a dry branch hanging to a withered tree that the wind moved to and fro. So when they had stayed there a long time their eyelids grew heavy with weariness, and they fell fast asleep.

When at last they woke it was night, and Gretel began to cry, and said, "How shall we ever get out of this wood?" But Hansel comforted her, saying, "Wait a little while longer, until the moon rises, and then we can easily find the way home." And when the full moon rose, Hansel took his little sister by the hand and followed the white stones that shone like silver and showed them the road.

They walked the whole night and at the break of day they came to their father's house. They knocked at the door, and when the wife opened it and saw that it was Hansel and Gretel she said, "You naughty children, why did you sleep so long in the wood? We thought you were never coming home again!" But their father was glad, for it had just about broken his heart to leave them in the woods alone.

A few nights later, the children heard their stepmother say to their father, "Everything is finished up; we have only half a loaf. The children must be taken farther into the wood this time, so that they shall not be able to find the way back again; there is no other way to manage." The man felt sad at heart, and he thought, "It would be better to share one's last morsel with one's children." But the wife would listen to nothing that he said. She scolded and reproached him instead.

When the parents had gone to sleep Hansel got up to go out and get more white stones, as he did before, but the wife had locked the door, and Hansel could not get out. He returned to bed and comforted his little sister. "Don't cry Gretel. I will find a way."

Early the next morning the wife came and pulled the children out of bed. She gave them each a little piece of bread and on the way to the wood Hansel crumbled the bread in his pocket, and often stopped to throw a crumb on the ground.

The woman led the children far into the wood, where they had never been before in all their lives. And again there was a large fire made, and their stepmother said, "Sit still, you children, and when you are tired you can go to sleep; we are going into the forest to cut wood, and in the evening, when we are ready to go home we will come and fetch you."

So when noon came Gretel shared her bread with Hansel. Then they went to sleep, and the evening passed, and no one came for the poor children. When they awoke it was dark night, and Hansel comforted his little sister, and said, "Wait a little, Gretel, until the moon gets up, then we shall be able to see the way home by the breadcrumbs that I scattered along the way."

So when the moon rose they got up, but they could find no crumbs of bread, for the birds of the woods and of the fields had devoured them. Hansel thought they might find the way all the same, but they could not. They went on all that night, and the next day from the morning until the evening, but they could not find the way out of the wood. They were very hungry, for they had nothing to eat but the few berries they could find. And when they were so tired that they could no longer drag themselves along, they lay down under a tree and fell asleep.

It was now the third morning since they had left their father's house. They were always trying to get back to it, but instead of that they only found themselves farther in the wood, and if help had not soon come they would have starved.

About noon they saw a pretty snow-white bird sitting on a bough and singing so sweetly that they stopped to listen. And when he had finished the bird spread his wings and flew before them, and they followed after him until they came to a little house. The bird perched on the roof, and as they came nearer they saw that the house was built of bread, the roof was made of cakes; and the window was of transparent sugar.

Hansel reached up and broke off a bit of the roof, just to see how it tasted, and Gretel stood by the window and gnawed at it.

Then they heard a thin voice call out from inside, "Nibble, nibble, like a mouse, who is nibbling at my house?"

And the children answered, "Never mind, it is the wind." and they went on eating.

Then the door opened, and an old woman came out, leaning upon a crutch. Hansel and Gretel felt very frightened and they dropped the food that they held. The old woman, however, nodded her head, and said, "Ah, my dear children, how come you are here? You must come indoors and stay with me. I'm sure you will be no trouble." So she took them each by the hand and led them into her little house.

There they found all kinds of delicious food and after they had stuffed themselves, the old woman showed them two little white beds. Soon they were asleep, dreaming sweet dreams.

Now what Hansel and Gretel did not know was that the old woman was actually a wicked witch who although her eyesight was failing, had a keen sense of smell. She had known the children were near because of that. And this witch was a child eater.

She watched the children sleeping and said to herself, "What a fine feast I will have as soon as I fatten up these children!"

Early in the morning, she grasped Hansel with her withered hand, and led him into a little stable, and shut him up behind a grating.

Then she went back to Gretel and shook her, crying, "Get up, lazy bones, fetch water, and cook something nice for your brother. He is outside in the stable and must be fattened up. And when he is fat enough I will eat him."

Gretel began to weep bitterly, but it was of no use, she had to do what the wicked witch told her to do.

Each morning the old woman visited the little stable, and cried, "Hansel, stretch out your finger, so I can tell if you are fat enough." Hansel, however, would hold out a little bone, and the old woman, with her weak eyes, could not see what it was, and supposing it to be Hansel's finger, wondered very much why it was not getting fatter.

When four weeks had passed and Hansel seemed to remain so thin, she lost patience and could wait no longer. "Now then, Gretel," she said to the little girl, "whether Hansel be fat or be he lean, tomorrow I must kill and cook him."

Early the next morning Gretel had to get up, make the fire, and fill the kettle. "First we will do the baking," said the old woman. "I have heated the oven already and kneaded the dough." She pushed poor Gretel towards the oven, and said, "Creep in and see if it is properly hot, so that the bread may be baked."

Now Gretel had the feeling that the old woman would shut the door behind her and eat her once she was baked. So she said, "I don't know how to do it: how shall I get in?"

"Stupid goose," said the old woman, "the opening is big enough. I could get in myself!" and she stooped down and put her head in the oven's mouth. Gretel gave her a push and she shut the iron door upon her. Oh how the old woman howled! But Gretel ran out the door and straight to Hansel, leaving the wicked witch to burn miserably.

Gretel ran to the stable and opened the grating, and cried, "Hansel, we are free! The old witch is dead!" The two hugged each other and laughed and danced about.

And as they had nothing more to fear they searched the old witch's house, and in every corner there stood chests of pearls and precious stones. Hansel filled his pockets and Gretel filled her apron with the jewels.

Then they left the witch's house. When they had journeyed a few hours they came to a great piece of water.

"We can never get across this," said Hansel, "I see no stepping-stones and no bridge."

"And there is no boat either," said Gretel; "but here comes a white duck, I will ask her if she will help us over." So she cried,

"Duck, duck, here we stand, Hansel and Gretel, on the land, stepping-stones and bridge we lack, carry us over on your nice white back."

The duck came over and Hansel got upon her and told his sister to come too. "No," answered Gretel, "that would be too hard upon the duck; we must go separately, one after the other." Once they crossed the water, they thanked the duck.

They kept walking until they came upon the wood that looked familiar. So they kept walking until at last they saw in the distance their father's home. They began running until they arrived at the door. They rushed in and hugged their father. He was overjoyed to see them for he thought they were surely dead.

Pulling away from their father and smiling, Gretel opened her apron and the pearls and precious stones scattered onto the floor. Their father's eyes widened. Then Hansel grinned and took out one handful after another out of his pocket. Their father's eyes widened even more. And the stepmother? Well, during their absence, she had died. And so, the woodcutter and his two children lived in great joy together.

Pleasant Ending

Well, it's kind of hard to top that original ending. How can you create a more pleasant ending than a father reunited with his children and now having plenty of money in the form of gems? But let's give it a try.

A few days after their return, Hansel and Gretel and their father, whose name was Hubert, fell into a routine. Gretel fixed their meals and Hansel and their father tidied up their small cabin.

With all their newfound riches, their father decided to purchase a new house in the nearest town – nothing too ostentatious- just a small cottage with three bedrooms.

Now his children would be able to go to school as well as spend time with other children. Hansel and Gretel were overjoyed. They made new friends quickly and did very well in school.

The woodcutter was, of course, no longer cutting wood, so he looked for something to occupy his time. He made what many of us would consider a natural segue from cutting wood to making one of a kind, custom wood furniture. And that is how Hubert met a woman just a few years younger than him named Hulda.

Hulda had visited the former woodcutter's, now a carpenter's, workshop which was in an outbuilding on their home's property to choose the wood she wanted made into a small table for her home. The two of them began talking and after the wood was chosen and a design discussed, they went into the house for coffee.

Hulda began spending more and more time, not only with Hubert, but with the children as well. She developed a great attachment to the man and the children, as they did to her. Now Hansel and Gretel's father did not want to rush things, after all his second marriage had been an utter failure, so he did not ask Hulda to marry him for nearly a year. And, he did not do this until after he discussed the possibility with his children.

Well, a year later there was a simple, but elegant wedding and Hulda became Hansel and Gretel's new stepmother. And all of them lived in great joy together.

Just Desserts Ending

A year later there was a simple, but elegant wedding and Hulda became Hansel and Gretel's new stepmother. During their courtship, Hulda had wondered how Hubert supported his family when he only made one piece of furniture at a time. However, there always seemed to be enough food in the home and the children had sufficient clothing and shoes, so she didn't concern herself too much about it.

However, once they had married, Hubert shared with Hulda that indeed, he did not support his family solely on his furniture business. He showed her the gemstones and shared the story of how his children had obtained them.

When Hulda saw those gems her eyes widened and her heart filled with desire – for the gems, not her new husband. And little by little she began to squirrel away a gem here and a gem there.

Since Hubert did not need to withdraw gems from his cache very often, he did not notice that the substantial pile of stones was getting smaller. One day he finished his day's work and went into the house, delighted to have some time to spend with his wife. But he could not find Hulda. He searched every room and called her name. But there was no response.

Hubert had seen Hansel and Gretel playing outside, so he went to them and asked, "Have you seen your mother?"

Both looked puzzled. "She gave us some milk and cake after school and sent us outside to play," replied Gretel.

They joined their father in searching the house, but there was no sign of Hulda. Hansel became suspicious and he opened the cupboard where their gems were kept. "Father! Father! Come quickly!" he called. Hubert gasped when he saw that only a small pile of gems was left in the cupboard. He raced to their bedroom and discovered that all of his wife's clothes were gone.

Once again a woman had hoodwinked him. But after all, when you marry a woman named Hulda, whose name means hiding and secrecy, what else could you expect?

But don't worry, between the gems that were left and Hubert's successful business, the family did not go hungry. But hopefully he learned that he did not have good sense when it came to women!

Now you might be wondering about Hulda. Well she established herself in another town, a much bigger town, far away. She used the gems to buy a house, beautiful furniture, magnificent gowns, and expensive jewelry.

She spent her days trying on different gowns and sitting in front of the mirror of her dressing table trying different hairstyles. Many men of various ages came a-courtin'. But they were not interested in Hulda for her magnificent gowns or her attractive hairstyles; they were interested in her money.

But Hulda had no business sense, and it wasn't long before the gems were gone. There was nothing left except her jewelry, gowns, furniture, and house. She began selling off items a bit at a time. This, of course, was noticed by those many men of various ages and they stopped asking Hulda out.

The last I heard, Hulda was working as a kitchen maid at an inn for room and board.

The Ugly Duckling

I t was a lovely summer day in the country and in a thicket by a slow-moving river sat a mother duck on her nest of eggs. She was tired of sitting on the eggs and wished they would hatch soon.

After a bit more time, the first egg cracked and soon all of her ducklings were out except the one from the largest of the eggs. An older female duck came by and admired the new, cute little ducklings. She advised the new mother to begin to teach her little ones how to swim since the unhatched egg was obviously a turkey egg.

A short time later, the large egg did hatch and out of it came a very large and quite ugly duckling. But this was one of her children and so the mother took him and the other ducklings to the farmyard to introduce them to the other birds who lived there and to teach them which animals to be leery of.

The biggest duckling was not well received. Some of the farm animals laughed at him and some nipped or pecked him. And then there were his brothers and sisters who said, "You are so ugly, we wish the cat would get you!"

The duckling ran away and spent his first night in the company of some wild ducks who said they didn't mind how ugly he was, as long as he didn't want to marry one of their females, which of course was the furthest thing from his mind.

After two days on the moor, two wild goslings came by and said to him. "You are so ugly, that we like you very well." And they invited him to join them.

But no sooner had these words left their beaks than a "pop, pop" was heard and the two goslings fell into the water. They had been shot by hunters.

The poor duckling was terrified. He hid his head under his wing just as a large, terrifying dog passed very near him. His jaws were open, his tongue hung from his mouth, and his eyes glared. He thrust his nose close to the duckling, showing his sharp teeth, but then he splashed into the water without touching him. The duckling sighed, "Oh, I'm thankful that I am so ugly that a dog will not bite me."

Still terrified, the duckling stayed in the water for hours, until he no longer heard the popping sounds or the splashing of the dog rushing through the water. He rushed out of the moor, raced through a field and a meadow until a storm arose. It was difficult to move in the strong wind, so he looked for shelter and found a poor little cottage that leaned so on one side he thought the strong wind might knock it down. But any port in a storm, right?

The duckling entered through the door, which was slightly ajar and made his way to a corner to dry off. Now that cottage was inhabited by an old woman, her beloved tom cat who she treated like a son, and her short-legged hen, who gave her eggs.

The next morning, the old woman was alerted to the existence of the duckling by her cat and hen. Her eyesight was so poor, she thought he was a fat duck who had wandered from home. She was thrilled to have some duck eggs, but after three weeks the ugly duckling had not laid a single egg. The cat and the hen suggested that he was worthless and needed to leave.

So the duckling left the cottage and soon found water on which it could swim and dive. All other animals avoided him, because of his ugly appearance. The glorious colors of autumn came and went and then it was winter.

The air was cold, and snow fell from the sky. The little duckling was very sad.

One evening as the sun was setting and coloring the sky with a reddish-orange glow, a large flock of beautiful birds came out of the bushes. They were swans, but the duckling did not know that. He admired their graceful necks and watched as they uttered a singular cry and spread their wings to mount higher and higher into the sky. He whirled himself in the water like a wheel, stretched out his neck towards them, and uttered a cry so strange that it frightened him.

The winter grew colder and colder. The duckling had to constantly swim about to keep the water from freezing. But eventually he became exhausted and lay still and help-less, frozen fast in the ice.

Early in the morning a passing peasant saw what had happened. He used his wooden shoe to break the ice and carried the duckling home to his wife. The warmth of the little house revived him, but the children, who wanted to play with him, frightened him. He raced around the room which caused the children to clap their hands and laugh. This frightened him more. As he knocked over the butter churn and a chair, the children's mother screamed and tried to grab him. The children tried to catch him, but he managed to slip out of the open door. Exhausted, he laid down behind some bushes in the newly fallen snow.

The winter was very harsh and hard for the duckling, but spring eventually came as it always does. The sun was warm on his wings, which felt strong, and so our young duckling flapped them against his sides and rose high into the air.

He found himself in a beautiful garden without quite understanding how that had happened. From a near-by thicket, came three beautiful white swans swimming lightly over the smooth water. He remembered the lovely birds and felt unhappier than he ever had.

He decided to approach them, even though they would probably kill him because he was so ugly. But to him it did not matter, for it would be better to be killed by such lovely birds than what he had endured.

So he flew to the water and swam towards the beautiful swans. They rushed to meet him with outstretched wings. And that's when he saw his own image in the clear water. He was no longer a dark, gray, ugly bird, but a graceful and beautiful swan. And now he had a new family, as the great swans swam around him and stroked his neck with their beaks. The ugly duckling now felt glad that he had endured sorrow and trouble, because it enabled him to better enjoy the pleasure and happiness around him now.

Pleasant ending

The ugly duckling, now a handsome swan, flourished with his new family. He mated with a lovely female, and they raised many children over the next few years.

Now you might think that he would teach his offspring to be spiteful toward ducks, but instead he taught them tolerance of all feathered animals no matter the color of their feathers or the "color" of their attitudes.

Just Desserts Ending

The ill treatment that ugly duckling received from his "brothers and sisters" was now a distant memory. And his former brothers and sisters? Well they learned that it isn't nice to treat others in such a manner. It was a harsh lesson.

They had told their brother that they wished the cat at the farmyard would "get" him and that was exactly the fate that awaited them. The sly cat waited with his litter mates until there was a dark night when the moon was just a sliver in the sky. They crept up on those ducks and ... well let's just say that nothing was left but some feathers on the riverbank. Karma can be a real .....

On another note, I do believe the farmer and his family enjoyed several delicious duck dinners over the next few weeks. The farmer was especially happy as he didn't have to waste any time away from his farm chores to hunt and he didn't have to use any of his ammunition, either. A win-win, wouldn't you say?

The Fisherman and His Wife

Once there was a fisherman and his wife who lived in a small, worn-out hut. The fisherman earned his living by fishing in the sea. Every morning he would arise early and take his little boat out. Sometimes he caught a few fish and so that would be their evening meal. Sometimes he would catch a few more fish and he would sell them at the market. But most often he came back with only one or even none.

His wife was not happy to be a fisherman's wife. She constantly nagged at him to get a better job so they could have a better house and eat better food and wear better clothes. He would smile at her and say there were people in worse situations and at least they had a roof over their heads and food to eat and clothes to wear. He was content with their life.

One day, the fisherman took his little boat out, put his line in the water and in moments felt a big tug. He reeled in his catch and found, to his surprise, a huge flounder. This was wonderful. Using his fish net, he hauled the flounder into the boat. He was delighted that a fish such as this would sell for a good price at the market. The fish looked at the fisherman and said, "Let me go, fisherman, for I am an enchanted fish. If you let me go, you will catch another fish today for your meal. And, in the future, you may call on me for a favor."

The fisherman could hardly believe his ears, but he did not hesitate, and threw the flounder back into the sea. As soon as the fish was out of sight another took its place in the net. Enough for a good supper, the fisherman thought and then he decided to head home to tell his wife about his wonderful fortune.

When he arrived home, his wife was happy to see the large fish he had brought but she was even more excited when he told her the story of the enchanted flounder.

"Did you ask the fish for a wish?"

"Well, no," he replied. "I didn't think of it. After all, he sent me this beautiful fish."

"Fish, fish," his wife responded. "We live in this miserable hut, and you're satisfied with a fish?!? Go back and ask him for a better house. A nice cottage with nice furniture."

The next morning, the fisherman took his little boat out on the sea. He called out to the fish, "Enchanted flounder in the sea, I have a wish, please come to me. My wife asks a favor of you, so to your promise, please be true."

Just as soon as the words left his lips, the flounder came to the boat and lifted his head out of the water. "What do you want from me?" it asked the fisherman.

"Well, it's actually my wife. She would like a nice house instead of the run-down hut we live in now."

"Go home," said the flounder. "Your wife will have what she wants."

When the man got home, the hut was gone. A beautiful new cottage stood in its place, with a white picket fence. The curtains and all the furniture were new, right down to the pots and pans. He couldn't believe his eyes. He asked his wife, "Are you happy now?"

She replied, "Perhaps."

A few weeks later the fisherman's wife told him the house was too small. "We need more room in the parlor, the kitchen is too cramped, and we need a bigger bedroom so we can have a bigger bed."

The fisherman replied, "I'm happy with our new cottage. It's fine for me."

"Well, it's not for me. Go back to the flounder and get us a manor house."

So the next morning, the fisherman got into his little boat and went out on the sea. He called out to the fish, "Enchanted flounder in the sea, I have a wish, please come to me. My wife asks a favor of you, so to your promise, please be true." Just as soon as the words left his lips, the flounder came to the boat and lifted his head out of the water.

"What do you want from me?" it asked the fisherman.

"Well, it's actually my wife. She would like a manor house. She says the cottage is too small."

"Go home," said the flounder. "Your wife will have what she wants."

When the man got home, the cottage was gone. A grand new house stood in its place. A servant opened the door. The walls were filled with paintings and tapestries. The furniture was made of fine oak. The dining room table was set with crystal glasses and plates made of silver. The fisherman felt out of place in this new house, but his wife seemed very pleased.

"Are you happy now?" he asked. "Perhaps," she replied.

A few weeks later this greedy woman was looking out the window of their grand home. She said, "Wouldn't it be nice if all the land as far as we could see was ours? Go tell the flounder that we want to be the king and queen of all these lands."

"What?!?" said the fisherman incredulously. "Have you gone mad? I do not wish to be king. I just want to be a fisherman."

"Fine," said his wife. "Then tell the flounder that I wish to be queen and live in a palace."

So the next morning, the fisherman slowly walked to his boat, slowly took the boat out to sea, and slowly called out to the flounder, "Enchanted flounder in the sea, I have a wish, please come to me. My wife asks a favor of you, so to your promise, please be true." Just as soon as the words left his lips, the flounder came to the boat and lifted his head out of the water.

It asked, "What does your wife want now?"

The tired fisherman said, "She wants to be queen of all the land she sees with a palace to live in."

"Go home," said the flounder. "Your wife will have what she wants."

When the fisherman arrived home, guards greeted him. A servant opened the door. There were servants everywhere. The inside of the palace was filled with gold objects.

There were fountains and gardens. Everything was huge, everything was opulent. His wife seemed very pleased.

The fisherman bravely asked her, "Are you happy now?"

Once again, she said, "Perhaps."

A few weeks later his wife was watching the sunset. She turned to her husband and said, "Being the queen is not enough. I want to be ruler of the universe. I want every person and every animal to bow before me. I want to make the sun rise and set and the stars shine. Go back to the flounder."

The frustrated fisherman went back to sea and called the flounder, "Enchanted flounder in the sea, I have a wish, please come to me. My wife asks a favor of you, so to your promise, please be true." Just as soon as the words left his lips, the flounder came to the boat and lifted his head out of the water.

It asked, "What does your wife want now?"

The extremely tired fisherman said, "She wants to be ruler of the universe and all living things. She wants to control the sun and the moon and the stars."

The flounder looked at the fisherman and said with a bit of a chuckle, "Go back to your wife. She has what she deserves."

When the fisherman got home the first thing he saw was his old hut. His spirits lifted and he went inside. There was his wife. The fisherman was pleased. As for his wife, if she was not pleased at least she was a bit wiser.

Pleasant Ending

The fisherman was pleased to be back in their hut. Indeed he was. As for his wife, she was not pleased. After all she had lost everything for which she had wished. But her husband was a good man and a good provider and so she didn't stay angry for long. Oh, she still got miffed at him from time to time, but not really, truly angry.

Now, her husband was well aware that a happy wife meant a happy life and so he began to put back a bit of money as often as he could. After a few years, or ten, he had enough money to build her a nice little cottage in the woods not too far from their little hut.

When it was finished, he covered her eyes with his handkerchief – even though she protested – and guided her into the woods. Then he removed her "blindfold". Now ten years had mellowed her disposition a bit and she took a long look at the cottage from right to left, left to right, from top to bottom, from bottom to top and proclaimed with a slight smile on her face, "It's good enough." And the fisherman decided that indeed, "It was good enough."

Just Desserts Ending

The fisherman was pleased with having his simple hut back, but his wife was not. However, she was a bit wiser and knew not to nag her husband about calling for the magic fish again. Besides, she had the feeling that the fish would not cooperate.

So she set her sights on something else. She told her husband that she would like to be in charge of taking his catch to the market. The fisherman was delighted that his wife wanted to be more involved in his business and agreed.

The fisherman's wife was a very astute businesswoman. She had had the feeling that her husband was undercharging for the fish and perhaps even giving some of his catch away. She had always felt he was too soft-hearted.

She asked top dollar for the fish and usually got it, but she did not tell her husband how much money she was collecting. Some of the money was used for household expenses, but most weeks she could also put some money back.

You might be wondering what she wanted the money for. Well she had a plan, a plan, I'm sorry to say to leave her husband. It took almost a year before she felt she had enough.

One warm, sunny autumn day while her husband was out fishing, she packed a bag, put the money she had hidden away into a pouch that she tucked inside her bag, and she started walking down the road.

She thought she would be able to get a ride from someone, but she hadn't seen a single soul and now after walking for miles her feet were getting sore.

She had just begun to doubt the soundness of her plan when she heard the sound of wagon wheels behind her. She moved over to the side of the road and looked up at the driver of the farm wagon.

He greeted her with a wide smile filled with snow-white teeth. She returned his smile. He reached his hand down to help her into the wagon and as he pulled her up, he hit her in the back of the head with the club he had in his other hand. Stunned, the fisherman's wife fell to the ground.

The driver of the wagon jumped down from his seat and rummaged through her bag until he found her pouch of money. Then smiling that wide smile filled with snow-white teeth, he climbed back onto the wagon, and called over his retreating shoulder, "Thank you."

And the fisherman's wife? Well, her head injury was quite severe and as she was blacking out she thought to herself "I should have known that a farmer wouldn't have such snow-white teeth." I'm sorry to relate that was the last thought that the fisherman's wife had as she succumbed to her injuries.

Now you are probably wondering about the fisherman. I'm sure he was quite upset when he returned home from fishing and found his wife's things missing, but he decided that it was probably for the best as his wife had never truly been happy being a fisherman's wife and living hand to mouth. He went to bed that night, and for many nights after that, hoping she had found what she was looking for and was finally happy.

The Elves and the Shoemaker

There was once a shoemaker, who although he was a hard worker and very honest, could not earn enough to live on. And there came a day when all he had left was just enough leather to make one pair of shoes.

That evening he cut the leather, all ready to make up the next day. His plan was to rise early in the morning to finish making the shoes. He went to bed and soon fell asleep.

In the morning he went into his workshop and sat down at his workbench to begin his work; but, to his great surprise, the shoes were already made. The shoemaker didn't know what to say or think at such an odd thing happening.

He looked at the workmanship and saw there was not one false stitch in the whole job. It was quite a masterpiece!

That same day a customer came in, and the shoes suited him so well that he willingly paid a price higher than usual for them. So the poor shoemaker was able to buy leather enough to make two pairs of shoes.

Once again in the evening he cut out the work, and went to bed early, planning to get up early the next morning and finish the shoes. And once again when he got up in the morning the work was done.

Several buyers came in that day, and they paid him handsomely for his goods. He was able to buy enough leather for four more pairs. He cut out the work again that night and found it done in the morning, as before.

This pattern continued for quite some time and soon the shoemaker and his wife had plenty of money and were doing well.

One evening, around Christmas, as he and his wife were sitting over the fire chatting, he said to her, "I should like to sit up and watch tonight, so I might see who it is that comes and does my work for me." The wife liked the idea; so they left a light burning and hid themselves behind a curtain in a corner of the room and watched what would happen.

As soon as it was midnight, two little naked dwarfs came in. They sat down upon the shoemaker's bench, took up all the work that was cut out, and began stitching and rapping and tapping away. They worked at such a rapid rate, that the shoemaker could not take his eyes off of them. The shoes stood ready long before daybreak; and then they bustled away as quick as lightning.

The next day the wife said to the shoemaker, "We should thank the little elves for helping us and I think I know how. I will make each of them a shirt, a coat, and a pair of pantaloons. You should make each of them a little pair of shoes."

The good cobbler liked the idea very much. So one evening, when all the things were ready, they laid them on the table, instead of the work that they used to cut out. Then went and hid themselves so they could watch what the little elves would do.

About midnight they came, dancing and skipping. Then they went to sit down to their work as usual; but when they saw the clothes set out for them, they laughed and chuckled, and seemed delighted. They dressed themselves in the twinkling of an eye, scampered around the room and danced out the door.

The good couple never saw them again, but everything went well with them from that time forward.

Pleasant Ending

But the story doesn't end there. The shoemaker and his wife were so grateful for their good fortune that they decided to find ways to help others in their community.

They did not want any thanks from the recipients of their gifts and so they delivered new shoes to needy children and adults in secret. Sort of like St. Nicholas.

And it warmed their hearts when they saw the joy and smiles on the faces of those recipients wearing their new shoes around the town. That was all the thanks the shoemaker and his wife needed.

Just Desserts Ending

But the story doesn't end there. The shoemaker and his wife were so grateful for their good fortune that they decided to find ways to help others in their community. They decided to secretly deliver new shoes to needy children and adults in their town.

The problem was finding a way to do that. Neither of them was slim enough to fit down a chimney – how did St. Nicholas do it? They, of course, did not have keys to other people's homes. So, the shoemaker and his wife spent many days thinking about how to accomplish their task.

Finally, they decided the best way would be to go to homes late at night and leave shoes on deserving people's doorsteps.

The first night came, and needless to say, they were very excited about the task at hand. They put on dark clothing to blend with the darkness of the night. Then they walked several blocks to the house where they are going to leave their first pair of shoes.

"My heart is pounding so hard, I'm afraid someone is going to hear it," the shoemaker's wife said quietly.

Her husband smiled at her and whispered, "I'm excited too, but I can't hear your heart."

But someone, or should I say something, did hear them.

As they approached the doorstep, they heard a deep, low growl. The family had a dog – a huge dog - and it was not happy to see them. The pair froze, uncertain what to do. And then the shoemaker remembered that he had a crust of bread from his dinner in his pocket. He never did like to eat the crusts and often hid them from his wife. He whispered to his wife, "Get ready to run." She nodded her head to show she understood.

The shoemaker threw the bread crust to the dog and he and his wife ran like their lives depended on it – and maybe it did. Once home, they reassessed their plan to be shoe fairies.

"Perhaps," his wife said, "we need to do some reconnaissance at the next house we are going to visit to make sure they don't have a dog." The shoemaker agreed.

Several nights later, once again dressed in dark clothes, the shoemaker and his wife walked to another house in their community. And just as they were about to leave a pair of shoes on the doorstep, they heard a voice call out, "Who's there? What are you doing here?"

Someone inside the house was still awake! Quite the night bird! The shoemaker and his wife turned and ran. Once they got home the shoemaker discovered he had not put the shoes on the doorstep and still had them in his hands.

"Oh no," the shoemaker said, holding up the shoes to show his wife. "This isn't going very well, is it?"

"No, it's not," his wife responded. "Let's go to bed, I'm exhausted."

Well the shoemaker and his wife did not try any deliveries for several weeks, after all they still had to make a living which meant spending time making shoes. And the late nights they had spent planning and attempting to execute their plans were hard on the old couple.

To be honest, they were becoming discouraged. But finally, they decided to try one last time. And so once again they donned dark clothes and headed into their community to their destination each carrying several pairs of shoes as they were going to a home on the edge of town in which lived not one, not three, but five children.

After a time, they reached the home of those five children. The ramshackle house looked like a strong wind would blow it over. They approached quietly, not even whispering for fear someone might hear them. They smiled at each other as they got to the doorstep and laid down five pairs of well-made shoes in various sizes.

Still smiling, delighted that they had finally been successful, the two turned to leave when they heard an eerie growling sound that was followed with hissing so loud they covered their ears. Suddenly they were being attacked by an animal that seemed to have a dozen paws with extremely long claws.

The shoemaker and his wife kept using their hands to try to push their attacker away and after what seemed like an eternity, the animal jumped down to the ground and raced away. They watched in amazement as they discovered they had been attacked by a large tabby cat.

Wearily they walked home. The shoemaker's wife got out iodine and bandages to take care of the scratches on their faces and hands. Once their wounds had been tended to, the two sat down to strong cups of tea. "I think we need to give up on this endeavor," the shoemaker's wife said. Her husband nodded his head in agreement and said, "No good deed goes unpunished." And that was the last clandestine night trip that they made. But they still made excellent shoes.

Puss in Boots

No book with fairy tales would be complete without including at least one Charles Perrault tale. And this is one of his many stories.

Once upon a time, there was a miller who left his three sons everything he had. And what did he have? Well, he had a mill, a donkey, and a cat. It didn't take long for them to split the inheritance. The oldest one took the mill, the middle one took the donkey, and the youngest one got the cat.

But what the older two sons didn't know was this wasn't any ordinary cat. This cat could talk. He told his master to get him a pair of boots and a bag. Soon the cat catches a rabbit and takes the rabbit to the king.

He tells the king that the rabbit is a gift from his master, better known as the Marquis of Carabas. The king loves the gift and sends the cat away telling him to thank his master. Over the next three months the cat brings the King more gifts of game, which he has caught, and tells the King they are from the Marquis of Carabas.

One day the king decides to take a carriage ride with his daughter, the lovely princess. When the cat learns of this, he tells his master to go and take a bath in the river and that he'll take care of the rest. So, the youngest son goes to the river. Puss hides his clothes under a rock and then, seeing the king's carriage approaching, starts shouting: "The Marquis of Carabas is drowning."

The king recognizes the cat, has the carriage driver stop, and he sends his men to help. While they are pulling the Marquis of Carabas out of the river, the cat tells the king that his masters' clothes were stolen while he was bathing. The king orders some of his men to go back to his castle and bring the finest clothes for the Marquis of Carabas. When the princess sees the miller's youngest son dressed in such finery, she immediately falls in love and invites him to join them in the carriage.

While they are heading to the king's castle, the cat goes ahead and tells the men who are working in the fields that they should say that the land belongs to the Marquis of

Carabas and if they don't obey him he will grind them into mincemeat. Scared, they tell the king when asked exactly as the cat directed. The fields, in actuality belong to an ogre.

Next, the cat goes to the castle where the ogre lives. Puss pretends to admire the ogre's ability to change himself into other creatures. First he changes himself into a lion. Puss applauds his ability, but then mentions that changing into something small would probably be too difficult. The ogre laughs and turns himself into a mouse and when he does the cat eats him.

Puss hears the king's carriage coming near the ogre's castle, so he goes out to greet them, telling them that they are in front of Marquis of Carabas' castle. The king is thrilled that in his kingdom lives such a rich Marquis and the princess is even more in love when she sees how rich he is.

The same day the king gives his permission for the two of them to get married. And Puss in Boots? Well, he becomes a real gentleman who chases mice for fun.

Pleasant Ending

Puss was made for a life of ease, but unlike some members of the upper class who overindulge in food and drink and spend their time lazing around, he did not. Well, wait, let me clarify. He did overindulge in rich foods from time to time, but he also did cardio every day. What kind of cardio, you ask. Well, Puss kept fit by chasing after the mice in the castle.

And boy were there a lot of mice! Soon Puss was devoting a lot of his day to chasing mice. This was more time than he wanted to commit to such a task. So the cat began looking around for a helper.

As it turns out there were plenty of choices for a mice-catching mate. The king himself had a beautiful, snow-white Persian. Puss went to see her, but it didn't take long for him to realize that although she was a great conversationalist, she was self-centered and had never caught a mouse in her life.

So Puss continued catching mice solo until he learned that there was a cat who lived in the alley behind the castle. Puss went to see her, but it didn't take long for him to realize that although she was a great mouser, she was gruff and rough and would never fit in at the castle. And she didn't want to talk about anything other than mousing styles.

Puss was beginning to give up hope of ever finding a helpmate but one day when he strolled down to the kitchen to get a little between-meal snack he saw her. She was curled up in a basket in front of the fireplace. A tiger cat with the longest whiskers he had ever seen.

He approached her and introduced himself. She reciprocated. They began to talk and soon discovered that they had many interests in common. That very afternoon they began "working out" together catching mice.

And Puss and his new friend, Katrina, lived happily ever after.

Just Desserts Ending

You are probably thinking there aren't any despicable characters in this story. Who deserves a just desserts ending? But think back to the beginning of the story. The miller died and left all he has to his three sons – the mill, a donkey, and a cat.

The three brothers could have shared the mill, donkey, and cat but no- the oldest brother took the mill, the middle brother took the donkey, and they left the cat for the youngest brother. Not a very fair deal, was it?

Well the older two brothers continued to operate the mill using the donkey to haul and carry. They did not treat the donkey well at all. If they didn't think he was moving fast enough – they beat him with a stick. If they didn't think he was carrying enough – they loaded on more.

After many months, the donkey had had enough and decided to leave. The donkey started walking down the road and just by chance ended up outside the King's castle.

The new prince, formerly known as the miller's youngest son, happened to be taking his daily constitutional and saw the donkey. And believe it or not, he recognized him.

Before you could say "hee-haw" the donkey found himself in the king's stables eating high quality hay and he got to live out the rest of his days in peace.

Without the donkey, the older brothers' work at the mill became more difficult. They were not very good money managers, so they had no money to buy a replacement donkey.

There were still a lot of things to haul and carry and they began to argue about who would carry them. The verbal argument spiraled into a physical fight and soon they were rolling on the ground delivering blows to each other's faces, ribs, and stomachs.

When they became too exhausted to deliver any more blows, they lay on the ground panting and wiping blood off their faces with their sleeves. They both realized this wasn't getting them anywhere.

They decided to ask a nearby farmer for the loan of his donkey, but he refused. He had seen how the boys had treated their donkey.

They went to a money lender hoping to get a loan so they could buy a donkey. But the money lender knew that the brothers had not been able to keep the mill running as efficiently as their father, so he refused.

So the brothers had to take turns being "the donkey" and they still spent every cent they made. They did not maintain the mill and it fell into disrepair. Customers, understandably so, began looking for other mills to hire.

Soon the brothers had no clients.

"One of us needs to work for someone else," said the oldest brother.

"It should be you," the middle brother replied.

"Me? Why me?"

"Well, being the oldest, you should look after me."

"Ha, that's a laugh! You should look after your elders."

"Oh yeah," said the middle brother. "Yeah!"

Well the next thing you know they were on the ground again delivering blows until they realized once again this wasn't getting them anywhere. In the end they both found jobs, but since they were not very skilled the pay was low and there was no extra money for things like taking a young lady out for a meal.

The last I heard, the two brothers are still single and living hand to mouth. But at least they have each other for company.

Part Two

Princess Stories

(Because, after all, what would a fairy tale book be without a few princess stories?)

Cinderella

There are thousands of Cinderella stories from around the world. One of my favorites is the one written by Charles Perrault in the late 1600's.

Cinderella's father, a nobleman and widower, remarries. His new wife is a very haughty and vain woman who has two daughters just like her. She has her new husband bamboozled and he is completely under her influence. Cinderella, on the other hand, is very sweet and kind. She is made to do all of the housework and sleeps in a garret, on a wretched straw bed, while her stepsisters get fine rooms with the most comfortable beds and large mirrors.

When she finishes all the work, she sits in the ashes, so everyone in the house calls her Cinderella. Even though her clothes are torn and tattered, and she is covered in cinders, she is still much more beautiful than her stepsisters, who are always nicely dressed.

One day, the young prince announces a royal ball. All the important people in the kingdom are invited, including Cinderella's two stepsisters. This just brings misery to Cinderella as she now not only has her regular chores, but also the job of making her stepsisters look as beautiful as possible. And to make things worse, her stepsisters tease Cinderella about not being able to go.

After they leave, Cinderella sits down in the ashes and begins to cry. Her fairy godmother appears and instructs Cinderella what to gather so she can go to the ball. A pumpkin becomes a coach, six mice become six horses and a rat becomes a coachman. Then her godmother touches her with her wand, and, in an instant, her clothes turn into cloth of gold and silver, all beset with jewels. This done, she gives Cinderella a pair of glass slippers. The prettiest shoes you have ever seen.

Cinderella goes to the ball after promising she will be home by midnight as that is when the magic will disappear. No one, not even her stepsisters, recognizes Cinderella as the mysterious princess and she spends a great deal of time with the prince. When she hears the clock tick fifteen minutes to midnight she quickly gets up from her seat, bows to everyone, and hurries to the exit. She makes it home before her stepsisters and listens to them tell about the mysterious, beautiful young woman who seems to have captured the prince's heart.

The ball continues the next night, but this time Cinderella is having so much fun she loses track of time and ends up walking the rest of the way home. In her rush to leave, one of her glass slippers drops and the Prince retrieves it. The prince announces that he will marry the girl to whom the glass shoe fits as he has fallen in love with a mysterious young lady. All the princesses and duchesses, and even the other girls in the court, try on the shoe, but it's all in vain.

One day the procession comes to Cinderella's house. Her two stepsisters try on the glass slipper, but they don't succeed. Cinderella asks if she can give it a go and since the man who has brought the slipper was told to have all young ladies in each household try, he agrees even as her stepmother and stepsisters are laughing about such an absurd idea.

Well, the shoe fits and Cinderella's godmother appears and waves her magic wand. Cinderella is immediately dressed from head to toe in gorgeous finery. She smiles and in case they still aren't convinced, she holds out the other glass slipper. Cinderella's stepsisters fall to their knees and beg her to forgive them for behaving badly towards her. Cinderella, who has always been good-hearted, hugs them and forgives them. She also says that she wants them to live in harmony.

They take Cinderella, so beautifully dressed, to the prince. After a few days, the prince and Cinderella get married – no sense in wasting any time, after all. Cinderella brings her stepsisters to the court, and on the same day, they marry two of the king's courtiers. I guess love isn't part of the equation.

But, you have to wonder, will the stepsisters become loving, good-hearted woman? After all, up to this point they've been self-centered and, let's face it, hateful. Zebras don't change their stripes and I have the feeling the step-sisters won't either.

And speaking of zebras not changing their stripes, life at the castle quickly becomes boring for our Cinderella. After all, there really isn't much for the new princess to do and she has such a strong work ethic. So, she begins checking in with the maids and before you can say "Prince Charming" she joins them in cleaning the castle. On any given day you could find her dusting the ornate wood furniture, sweeping the long marble tiled hallways, or hanging carpets outside and beating the living daylights out of them – or at least all the dust. Now don't get me wrong, it's not that she really enjoys cleaning, but it helps her pass the time and helps her feel useful.

It takes a while for her hubby, Prince Charming, to notice her activities and I have to say, he is not happy about it. Dusting, sweeping, and beating carpets is just not something princesses do. He forbids his bride to continue working with the maids.

For a few weeks Cinderella goes back to being a beautiful, but bored out of her mind, princess. One afternoon she wanders into the kitchen. Cook is bustling around, jumping from one thing to another preparing dinner for the royal family. Her assistant had left her position to get married and Cook hasn't had time to replace her yet. Cinderella offers her help.

Cook replies, "Oh no, your Majesty. I'll manage."

To which Cinderella responds as she picks up a paring knife and begins cutting carrots, "Nonsense, you need help, and I am a good hand in the kitchen." And from then on, Princess Cinderella appears in the kitchen every afternoon and lends Cook a hand.

Once again it takes a while for her hubby, Prince Charming, to notice her activities. And once again, he is not happy about her helping in the kitchen and explains that this too is not something princesses do. As you can imagine, Cinderella is a bit ticked off. I'm not sure which makes her the angriest – the fact that the Prince takes so long to notice what she has been doing or that he keeps forbidding her to do things.

So, Cinderella confronts her husband and explains that she needs to feel useful and continuing to be forbidden to do things is getting old. Her husband smiles his million-dollar, bright white smile and suggests that she finds something she enjoys doing that doesn't involve her helping the staff do their work.

What to do, what to do, the princess ponders. Now you might not know this about Cinderella, but she has always had a way with animals – think about the birds and other animals that help her in the Disney cartoon version – and so she begins a foster program for the stray cats and dogs she finds on the castle grounds. And so the history of royalty doing charitable works begins.

But that is not the only way Cinderella is a trailblazer. She asks her Fairy Godmother to sit with her and Prince Charming as they iron out some issues, like him "forbidding" her to do things. Although the Prince is concerned at first that the Fairy Godmother will be biased toward Cinderella, he soon discovers she is fair and does not take sides. And so the Fairy Godmother becomes the first marriage counselor.

Prince Charming and Princess Cinderella learn to respect each other's differences and how to compromise – after all that is how marriages succeed and survive - and they lived happily ever after.

Postscript: Now, you might be wondering about the two stepsisters- especially since I intimated they might not be able to change their ways. I'm going to offer you a choice of endings for those two. Pleasant Ending or Just Desserts – the choice is yours.

Pleasant Ending

Well, I'm happy to report that although they didn't exactly become loving, good-hearted women, the two stepsisters were pleasant enough. After all, they were now members of the court and their only responsibilities were to wear stunning gowns, wear beautiful wigs, wear plastered on smiles, and make pleasant conversation. They managed these responsibilities easily - well, the conversation was a bit self-centered - but otherwise it was if they were born to be the wives of courtiers!

And so, the two stepsisters, and hopefully their husbands as well, also lived happily ever after.

Just Desserts

We know that the two stepsisters were haughty, vain, and self-centered. Do you think they became reformed characters just because they married members of the court? Hardly.

To make things easier, I'm going to name the two stepsisters. Since my childhood view of Cinderella was shaped by watching Rodgers and Hammerstein's 1965 television version with Leslie Ann Warren, I'm going to use those stepsisters' names – Prunella and Esmerelda.

Let's start with Esmerelda. She was very proud of her slender figure and was actually the same size as Cinderella. She admired Cinderella's beautiful, one-of-a-kind gowns, even though she had lovely gowns of her own. Esmerelda had even asked Cinderella if she could wear one of her gowns, but Cinderella has explained that they are made just for her but adds that she'd be happy to have the royal dressmaker design and create a dress just for Esmerelda. Needless to say, Esmerelda was not satisfied with that response. She wanted to wear a dress that a princess has worn.

So, she sneaked into Cinderella's dressing room and began to sabotage the gowns. How, you ask? Well, in numerous ways. One exquisite emerald green gown's skirt is covered with small pearls. Esmerelda loosens the strings that hold the pearls so that when Cinderella next wears it, the pearls will fall off.

And that is exactly what happened. Just a few days later, the King and Queen hosted a ball celebrating, celebrating ... well it doesn't really matter, does it? The point is there was a ball and Cinderella wore her new exquisite emerald green gown. She and the Prince went onto the dance floor and began waltzing. Pearls began falling off her gown, unnoticed at first. But then a few members of the court and other guests began stepping on the pearls and it caused some of them who were not as steady on their feet – perhaps too much wine- to fall. No one was seriously injured, but tucked behind an ornate screen, Esmerelda laughed so hard tears rolled down her cheeks and onto her own lovely gown.

But that wasn't enough for Esmerelda. Cinderella also had a gorgeous grape-colored gown with a bodice covered in diamonds that sparkled even in a dimly lit room.

Esmerelda was especially fond of this dress as she felt purple was her color and she was very fond of diamonds, as well. She hesitated at first, reluctant to damage such a beautiful dress, but since she knew she would never be allowed to wear it, she took a deep breath and used a knife to deftly cut slits into the skirt of the dress. The next time

Cinderella wears it, she will be embarrassed as will Prince Charming, thought Esmerelda.

But it was not to be. You see, servants are often overlooked or ignored in castles. And one of these servants had noticed Esmerelda go into the Princess's dressing room. She watched in horror as Esmerelda used her knife on the gorgeous gown. She quietly left the room and ran swiftly to Cinderella's maid in waiting.

Before you could say, "Uh oh, Esmerelda's in trouble", she was. Her punishment? She was condemned to work as a maid and wear the clothes of a peasant.

Now we come to Prunella. Prunella did not have the slim figure of her sister or of Cinderella. One of the reasons was because she was born big boned, but the other was because Prunella enjoyed food. She had no favorite victuals. Meats, breads, fruits, cakes ... she loved them all!

Needless to say, she had no aspirations to wear any of Cinderella's gowns. However, she did envy some of the special dishes that the chef made for the royal family. She felt that as a member of the court, she should have access to the same dishes. If she had asked Cinderella, she probably would have been happy to instruct the chef to provide Prunella with those delicacies, but Prunella never expressed her wishes to anyone. Instead, she decided to take matters into her own hands.

Prunella "borrowed" the dress of the plump head housemaid and covered her head with a scarf. Then she visited an old woman who was known for her herbal medicines and potions. Prunella told her that she was having trouble with an invasive weed that had taken over her vegetable garden and required a poison to kill the weed.

The old woman gave her a small brown bottle with the caution that the poison in the bottle was strong and to use it sparingly. Prunella promised her to be careful, thanked her and left.

Prunella, still disguised, slipped into the kitchen, and made her way to the prep table. She began cutting up carrots as she watched the chef prepare that evening's meal for the royal family. When the chef stepped away from the soup to check on the meat roasting in the fireplace, Prunella surreptitiously poured the entire contents of the small brown bottle into the soup. Then she slipped out of the kitchen to dress for dinner.

Imagine how Prunella felt as she sat at the table with her husband and watched the royal family, who sat at their table on the dais, sipping their soup. Was she nervous? Excited? Both?

But nothing happened. Nothing at all. Prunella kept watching and watching. The royal family finished their soup and sent their compliments to the chef. Maybe the poison took a while to work, thought Prunella. The next course was served and consumed. Still nothing happened. She couldn't believe it! The old woman had warned her that the poison was very potent. What had gone wrong? Do you know?

You see, Prunella had forgotten something very important. Fairy godmothers keep a watchful eye on you, all your life. That old woman? She was Cinderella's fairy godmother. The small brown bottle? Filled with nothing more than water.

The fairy godmother didn't want to be a tattle tale, but trying to poison the royal family could not be tolerated. She let Cinderella and Prince Charming know what Prunella had attempted to do.

I suppose you'd like to know Prunella's punishment. Well, she was assigned to kitchen clean up duty and spent her days washing and drying all the glasses and dishes used by the royal family and the members of the court.

A bit ironic, isn't it? Both the stepsisters ended up doing the work that once upon a time they used to force Cinderella to do.

The Princess and the Pea

H ans Christian Andersen authored this story about a prince's search for a princess to wed. He searches far and wide all over the world but is never quite sure if the women he finds are actual princesses. So he returns home to his parents' palace very discouraged.

One evening a terrible storm arises, with thunderous thunder and lightning strikes too numerous to count. The rain quickly becomes a torrential downpour and it is as dark as pitch. All at once there is a violent knocking at the door, and the old King, the Prince's father, goes to open it.

Standing on the cobblestones is a young lady in a sad condition. Water is trickling down from her hair, and her clothes cling to her body. She asks if she might come in and get dried off. The King lets her in and in conversation she reveals that she is a princess. The King informs his wife that a princess has arrived at the doorstep.

"We'll see about that," the Queen responds, and she has the guest room prepared in a unique way. In some versions of the story, she puts a single pea under twenty mattresses over which she puts twenty feather beds. In other versions, she puts three peas under them.

Since it is quite late, the household retires to their bed chambers. The Princess has been given dry night clothes to wear and she begins to climb up to the top of the mattresses. Did she find it odd that there were so many mattresses? We will never know.

The next morning she is asked how she slept. "Oh, very badly indeed!" she replies. "I scarcely closed my eyes the whole night through. I do not know what was in my bed, but I had something hard under me. Now I am black and blue all over. There are bruises on my bruises!"

Now it is plain that the lady must be a real princess since she had been able to feel the little pea or peas through the twenty mattresses and twenty feather beds. Only a real princess could have such a delicate sense of feeling.

The Prince accordingly makes her his wife; being now convinced that he has found a real Princess. The pea, or peas, are put into the cabinet of curiosities, where it, or they, remain to this day, unless, of course, it, or they, have been lost.

Well, that's the story, more or less, the way Mr. Andersen wrote it. But is it the true story?

Let's go back to the moment when the King opens the door on that dark, stormy night.

The King, who although old has excellent eyesight, realizes that the drenched young lady standing before him is quite comely, dare I say beautiful. Perhaps she could be a match for his son, he thinks to himself.

The King, who although old is quite wise, feels his son's gallivanting around looking for a princess to wed has been a waste of time. After all, there are plenty of lovely, available young ladies right here in his kingdom and the King is not as committed to the queen's and prince's notions that the prince must marry a princess.

Remember the conversation the King had with the young lady during which she said she was a princess? Well, the young lady, whose name was Rebecca, had admired the prince from a distance for years and had fallen in love with him. Her life was a hard one, as she had been on her own since she was a lass of just fourteen. Rebecca had been supporting herself by working long hours in a tavern, waiting on tables, clearing up, and cleaning. Her hands were constantly red, and her feet were always sore and throbbing. When she heard that the prince had returned home, she devised a plan to meet him.

She waited for a stormy night, knowing a drenched young lady would be given refuge at the castle. Being on her own for so long, she had developed the ability to lie with ease. But the King, who although old was perceptive, knew that she was not telling the truth. She was not a princess. But as I said before, he wasn't concerned about his son marrying royal blood.

So the sly King watched as his wife put the pea under the twenty mattresses and twenty feather beds that the staff brought into the guest room. When she leaves the room, the King, who although old is very clever, uses the lance from one of their knights as a lever to raise the twenty mattresses and twenty feather beds and puts several huge fieldstones under them ensuring that the young lady will not be able to sleep well.

So that brings us to the original ending of the story, which is more or less what happened. The Prince and "Princess" get married. But do the Princess and Prince live happily ever after? Hmm... a momma's boy marries an independent young lady. What do you think?

Pleasant Ending

As with all newlyweds, there are things that need to be worked out, after all, these are two people living together for the first time. But instead of discussing things with his wife, the Prince goes to the Queen Mother. Turns out the Prince is constantly at his mother's side asking and taking her advice about everything. Well, the Princess gets sick and tired of it and demands a trial separation.

Since the castle was huge, Rebecca didn't actually have to move out but took up residence in the east wing. She has a lovely bedroom with an attached sitting room and her meals are delivered to her. The King visits her daily and brings her news of what's going on in the castle as well as keeping her supplied with books to read from the castle's extensive library.

Now I'm not saying that Rebecca didn't miss Prince Michael, but she was enjoying having all of this time to herself – something she'd never had before. She read those books voraciously and discovered that she could remember every detail, every fact. She also enjoyed getting to know her father-in-law better. The King loved his wife, but as the years passed, she had become more and more domineering. They bonded over their mixed feelings for her.

The days turned into weeks, the weeks into months, and after a few months Princess Rebecca realized that she was expecting a child. Having come from a broken home herself, she didn't want that for her child. She decides to take steps to determine if Prince Michael could break away from his mother's apron strings and become the husband she wanted and the father their child deserved.

She began inviting Prince Michael to come to her sitting room. She entertains him with stories – some from the books she's read and some from experiences she has had while working at the tavern – of course she doesn't tell him the origin of those stories. Rebecca also asks him his opinion about things – unimportant things at first and gradually more important topics.

It takes a few months, but the Prince realizes that he does have his own opinions and can make decisions without consulting his mother. He truly becomes a partner in his marriage to Princess Rebecca.

The last I heard, they are still living happily ever after and will celebrate their 50th wedding anniversary at a huge party with their children, grandchildren, and friends.

Just Desserts Ending

Somehow several months later the Queen Mother discovers that Princess Rebecca was not a princess before she married the Prince. Perhaps one of the servants found the field stones that the King had put under the mattresses. Perhaps a member of the royal court mentioned having seen Rebecca working at the tavern. But it doesn't really matter how she found out. Smiling with her newfound knowledge, the Queen decides to tell her son.

Now as I mentioned, Prince Michael had always been a bit of a momma's boy, but he has fallen madly in love with his wife, and she has just told him that she is expecting their child. And, you might recall, the King, who is old but wise, doesn't always see eye to eye with his wife either.

The family always ate their evening meal together at 8:00 sharp in the royal dining room. They were sitting around the twelve-foot table eating their first course of delicious soup when the Queen picked up her spoon and tapped it lightly on her wine glass. They each put their spoons down and looked over at the Queen.

"I have an announcement to make," declared the Queen. The King, Prince Michael, and Princess Rebecca gave her their full attention. The Queen looked at each of them in turn and then focused on Rebecca. Pointing at Rebecca with her right index finger she stated, "She is not a princess!"

The King looked down at his lap, Rebecca turned red, but Prince Michael said, "What are you talking about, Mother? Of course she's a princess. We are married."

The Queen glared at her son and said, "I mean before you married. She was not a princess. She WORKED! She WORKED at a tavern."

Prince Michael smiled at his mother and said, "Yes, I know, Mother."

"You...you...you know?" his mother spluttered.

"Of course, Rebecca told me."

"She told you? She told you?"

"Yes, she told me," Prince Michael replied.

"And you are all right with this?" she asked.

"Well, I will admit I was surprised at first, but she is a princess now, so it doesn't really matter." His mother was speechless – a rarity for sure.

"And, Mother and Father, we have an announcement to make," Prince Michael said smiling at Princess Rebecca who nodded her approval. The King looked at his son and daughter-in-law expectantly. "There will be a baby in the spring." The King clapped his hands with joy and jumped up to hug them.

A hideous groaning sound escaped from the Queen's mouth. "The grandmother of a peasant's child!" she wailed as she stormed out of the room.

From that time on, the Queen occupied another wing of the house and was rarely seen. And, if I'm being honest, it made for a much happier household.

Snow White

Once upon a time, long, long ago a king and queen ruled over a distant land. The queen was kind and lovely and all the people of the realm adored her. The only sadness in the queen's life was that she wished for a child but did not have one.

One winter day, the queen was doing needle work while gazing out her ebony window at the new fallen snow. A bird flew by the window startling the queen and she pricked her finger. A single drop of blood fell on the snow outside her window. As she looked at the blood on the snow she said to herself, "Oh, how I wish that I had a daughter that had skin as white as snow, lips as red as blood, and hair as black as ebony."

Soon after that, the kind queen got her wish when she gave birth to a baby girl who had skin white as snow, lips red as blood, and hair black as ebony. They named the baby princess Snow White, but sadly, the queen died after giving birth to Snow White.

Soon after, the king married a new woman who was beautiful, but also proud and cruel. She had studied dark magic and owned a magic mirror, of which she would daily ask, "Mirror, mirror on the wall, who's the fairest of them all?"

Each time this question was asked, the mirror would give the same answer, "Thou, O Queen, art the fairest of all." This pleased the queen greatly as she knew that her magical mirror could speak nothing but the truth.

One morning, many years later, when the queen asked, "Mirror, mirror on the wall, who's the fairest of them all?" she was shocked when it answered: "You, my queen, are fair; it is true. But Snow White is even fairer than you."

The Queen flew into a jealous rage and ordered her huntsman to take Snow White into the woods to be killed. She demanded that the huntsman return with Snow White's heart as proof.

The poor huntsman took Snow White into the forest but found himself unable to kill the girl. Instead, he let her go, and brought the queen the heart of a wild boar.

Snow White was now all alone in the great forest, and she did not know what to do. She ran as far as her feet could carry her. Early in the evening she saw a little house, and, being very weary, went inside in order to rest.

Inside the house everything was small but tidy. There was a little table with a clean, white tablecloth and seven little plates. Against the wall there were seven little beds, all in a row and covered with quilts.

Because she was so hungry Snow White ate a few vegetables and a little bread from each little plate and she drank a bit of milk from each cup. Afterward, she lay down on one of the little beds and fell fast asleep.

After dark, the owners of the house returned home. They were the seven dwarfs who mined for gold in the mountains. As soon as they arrived home, they saw that someone had been there -- for not everything was in the same order as they had left it.

Looking around their home, they found Snow White lying asleep in the seventh bed. They cried out in amazement.

They were so happy that they did not wake her up but let her continue to sleep in the bed. The next morning Snow White woke up, and when she saw the seven dwarfs she was frightened. But they were friendly and asked, "What is your name?"

"My name is Snow White," she answered.

"Where did you come from?" the dwarfs asked her. She told them her story.

The dwarfs spoke with each other for a while and then said, "If you will keep house for us, and cook, make the beds, wash, sew, and knit, and keep everything clean and orderly, then you can stay with us." Snow White agreed to the arrangement and they lived happily together. However, it does make you wonder how Snow White knew how to do all these things, doesn't it?

Every morning the dwarfs went into the mountains looking for gold, and in the evening when they came back home Snow White had their house tidy and their evening meal was ready. During the day, the girl was alone, except for the small animals of the forest that she often played with.

Now the queen, believing that she had eaten Snow White's heart, could only think that she was again the most beautiful woman of all. She stepped before her mirror and said: "Mirror, mirror, on the wall, who's the fairest of them all?"

It answered: "You, my queen, are fair; it is true. But Snow White, beyond the mountains with the seven dwarfs, is still a thousand times fairer than you."

This startled the queen, for she knew that the mirror did not lie, and she realized that the huntsman had deceived her. Snow White was still alive! So she set out to devise a plan of how she could rid herself of Snow White.

She went into her secret room -- no one else was allowed inside -- and she made a poisoned apple. From the outside it was beautiful, and anyone who saw it would want it. But anyone who might eat a little piece of it would die. She disguised herself as an old peddler woman, so that no one would recognize her, traveled to the dwarfs' house, and knocked on the door.

Snow White put her head out of the window, and said, "I must not let anyone in; the seven dwarfs have forbidden me to do so."

"That is all right with me," answered the peddler woman. "I'll easily get rid of my apples. Here, I'll give you one of them."

"No," said Snow White, "I cannot accept anything from strangers."

"Are you afraid of poison?" asked the old woman. "Look, I'll cut the apple in two. You eat half and I shall eat half." The apple had been so artfully made that only one half was poisoned. Snow White longed for the beautiful apple, and when she saw that the peddler woman was eating part of it she could no longer resist, and she stuck her hand out and took the poisoned half. She barely had a bite in her mouth when she fell to the ground dead.

The queen looked at her with an evil stare, laughed loudly, and said, "White as snow, red as blood, black as ebony wood! The dwarfs shall never awaken you."

Back at home she asked her mirror, "Mirror, mirror, on the wall, who is the fairest of them all?"

It finally answered, "You, my queen, are fairest of all."

When the dwarfs came home that evening they found Snow White lying on the ground not breathing. They talked to her, shook her, and wept over her. But nothing helped. The dear child was dead, so they laid her on a bed of straw, and all seven sat next to her and mourned for her and cried for three days.

They could not find it in their hearts to bury her in the ground, so they had a glass coffin made with her name written in gold letters on the side. They put the coffin outside on a mountain, and one of them always stayed with it and watched over her. The animals came too and mourned for Snow White.

Now it came to pass that a prince entered the woods where the dwarfs' house was. He saw the coffin on the mountain and read what was written on it. He immediately fell in love with the beautiful Snow White.

He offered to buy the coffin, but the dwarfs responded that they would not sell it for all the gold in the world. So he asked if they would give him the coffin. "I cannot live without being able to see Snow White. I will honor and cherish her."

The dwarfs felt pity for him and decided to give him the coffin. The prince had his servants carry it away on their shoulders. As they were carrying the coffin, one of them stumbled and dislodged the piece of poisoned apple that Snow White had bitten off. She opened her eyes, lifted the lid from her coffin, and sat up.

"Where am I?" she cried out.

The prince said joyfully, "You are with me." He told her what had happened, and then said, "I love you more than anything else in the world. Come with me to my father's castle. You shall become my wife." Snow White loved him, and she went with him. A splendid wedding was planned, and all of the kingdom was invited to the feast. This, of course, included Snow White's stepmother.

Her stepmother adorned herself with beautiful garments, stood before her mirror, and said, "Mirror, mirror, on the wall, who is the fairest of them all?"

The mirror answered, "You, my queen, are fair; it is true. But the young queen is a thousand times fairer than you."

Not knowing that this new queen was indeed her stepdaughter, she arrived at the wedding, and when she saw Snow White, she flew into a rage! The king's guards subdued the evil queen, and she was banished from the kingdom. The prince and Snow White lived happily ever after.

Pleasant Ending

Now some people say that a leopard can't change its spots, but that did not prove true for the evil queen, Queen Grimhilde.

The guards took Grimhilde to a faraway cabin situated on top of a mountain. The cabin had been used, once upon a time, as a hunting lodge for the King and Prince when the Prince was much younger. It still had some basic supplies. Grimhilde was forced to live simply not only because of the meagerness of the supplies, but also because her sources of power, her magic mirror and secret room, were far, far away.

Without her magic and no servants, Grimhilde had to tend to everything herself. Her soft, white hands roughened a bit. Her artificial beauty faded but it was replaced with a natural look that quite suited her. And since she had no way to continue dying her hair stark black her natural cognac brown hair grew back.

Being alone gave her a lot of time to think. She thought about how badly she had treated the people in her life, especially Snow White. She thought about how lonely her life was now and had always been. She thought about how to change her situation.

One warm spring day several years later, Grimhilde decided to trek back to the King's castle and ask for Snow White's forgiveness. It took her weeks, and the journey was not an easy one. She fell many times, tore her clothes, twisted an ankle, and bruised herself in several places. But she persisted.

With the change in her looks and her torn clothes, she was unrecognizable when she reached the castle. She was sent away from the front gate and sent around the back to the servants' entrance. There the kindly cook let her into the kitchen and brought her a strong cup of tea and a plate of delicious cakes. She sat down with Grimhilde and asked her if she was looking for work.

Now the old Grimhilde would have flown into a rage, but the new Grimhilde smiled and replied that she was actually seeking an audience with the new queen. The cook said, "Well dearie, most afternoons about this time she goes into the gardens. Why don't we take a stroll there now."

And that is how Grimhilde was able to speak with Snow White. It was also how she discovered that she was now a grandmother.

So Grimhilde asked Snow White for her forgiveness. Snow White saw the changes in her stepmother and since she had always had a good heart she agreed to give her stepmother a second chance. The Prince was a bit harder to convince. He insisted that they spend time together over the next few months before he agreed to let her back into their lives.

So they all lived happily ever after.

Just Desserts Ending

The guards took Grimhilde to a faraway cabin situated on top of a mountain. The cabin had been used, once upon a time, as a hunting lodge for the King and Prince when the Prince was much younger. It still had some basic supplies. At first, Grimhilde was forced to live simply not only because of the meagerness of the supplies, but also because her main sources of power, her magic mirror and secret room, were far, far away.

But Grimhilde still had a trick or two up her sleeves. She was well versed in the arts of using natural roots and such to conjure, but she hadn't done any conjuring without consulting her books in a long while. For weeks she racked her brain for the ingredients needed to change a woman into a man. Her idea was to change herself into a handsome young man and entice Snow White outside the castle walls. Once out of sight of the guards, Grimhilde planned to plunge a knife into Snow White's heart and rid her of the young woman's greater beauty once and for all.

Finally Grimhilde remembered the needed ingredients and how to prepare the potion. It took her several days to locate everything she needed. She was grateful that the small cabin was well supplied with pots, pans, and cooking utensils.

She rolled up her sleeves and went to work. She was very excited about the prospect of ridding herself of Snow White once and for all as well as being able to return to her own castle. She actually hummed as she went to work.

After a few hours, the potion was ready. She rooted around the cabin and found a change of clothing that had been left behind by the King. She changed into the men's clothing, stuffed her long hair under a man's cap and poured the potion into a cup.

She took a long drink of the liquid, which burnt her throat a bit as it went down. But, she said aloud, "A little pain is worth the SNORT. Worth the SNORT."

Those were the last words Grimhilde said, at least the last words in English. Somehow she had not remembered the ingredients correctly or maybe she had not remembered the correct procedure, but it didn't really matter. For now Grimhilde was a hog. And not just any hog, a wild hog. "SNORT, SNORT."

I don't think the remainder of her days were quite what she expected, do you?

Sleeping Beauty

I n times past there lived a king and queen, who desperately wanted a child. But one day when the queen was bathing, there came a frog out of the water, and he said to her: "Thy wish shall be fulfilled; before a year has gone by, thou shalt bring a daughter into the world."

And just as the frog had said, the queen gave birth to a beautiful daughter. The king declared that he was going to give a great feast. He invited relatives, friends, acquaintances, and the wise women, hoping they would be kind and favorable to the child. There were thirteen of them in his kingdom, but as he had only provided twelve golden plates for them to eat from, one of them had to be left out.

The feast was celebrated with all splendor; and as it drew to an end, the wise women stood forward to present to the child their wonderful gifts: one bestowed virtue, one beauty, a third riches, and so on. And when eleven of them had said their say, in came the uninvited thirteenth.

She was outraged and wanted revenge, so without greeting or respect, she shouted loudly: "In the fifteenth year of her age the princess shall prick herself with a spindle and shall fall down dead." And without speaking one more word she turned away and left the hall.

Everyone was terrified and the queen began to weep. But the twelfth wise woman, who had not yet bestowed her gift, came forward. She explained that she could not do away with the evil prophecy, but she could soften it. She said: "The princess shall not die but fall into a deep sleep for a hundred years."

The king was determined that the prophecy would not come to pass. He gave commandment that all the spindles in his kingdom should be burnt up. The maiden grew up, adorned with all the gifts of the wise women; and she was so lovely, modest, sweet, and kind and clever, that no one who saw her could help loving her.

One day, shortly after her fifteenth birthday, her parents took a trip, and the princess was alone in the castle. She wandered about into all the nooks and corners, and into all the chambers and parlors. At last she came to an old tower. She climbed the narrow winding stair which led to a little door, with a rusty key sticking out of the lock. Curious, she turned the key, and the door opened, and there in the little room sat an old woman with a spindle, diligently spinning her flax.

"Good day, mother," said the princess, "what are you doing?"

"I am spinning," answered the old woman, nodding her head.

"What thing is that that twists round so briskly?" asked the maiden and she reached out to touch it. No sooner had she touched it than the evil prophecy was fulfilled, and she pricked her finger with it. She fell onto the floor into a deep sleep. Cackling, the old woman picked up the spinning wheel with the agility of a much younger woman and left the castle.

This sleep fell upon the whole castle. The king and queen, who had returned and were in the great hall, fell fast asleep, and with them the whole court. The horses in their stalls, the dogs in the yard, the pigeons on the roof, the flies on the wall, the fire that flickered in the fireplace, became still, and slept like the rest, even the meat on the spit ceased roasting. The wind ceased, and not a leaf fell from the trees about the castle. A hedge of thorns grew around the castle and became thicker every year. The whole castle became hidden from view, and nothing of it could be seen but the vane on the roof.

Word of a beautiful sleeping princess, named Rosamond, traveled throughout the land. From time to time many kings' sons came and tried to force their way through the hedge; but it was impossible for them to do so, for the thorns held fast together like strong hands. The young men were caught by them, and not being able to get free, died horrible deaths.

Many years afterwards there came a king's son into that country. He heard the story being told by an old man about a castle standing behind the hedge of thorns, and that there a beautiful enchanted princess named Rosamond had slept for a hundred years, and with her the king and queen, and the whole court. The old man had been told the story by his grandfather and added that many kings' sons had tried to breach the hedge of thorns, but all had died trying.

The young man said that he wanted to try his luck so he would have the chance to see the lovely Rosamond. The old man tried to dissuade him, but he would not listen.

As it happened, the hundred years were at an end, and the day had come when Rosamond should be awakened. When the prince drew near the hedge of thorns, it was changed into a hedge of beautiful large flowers, which parted and bent aside to let him pass, and then closed behind him in a thick hedge.

When he reached the castle-yard, he saw the horses and hunting-dogs lying asleep, and the pigeons asleep on the roof. When he came indoors, the flies on the wall were asleep, the cook in the kitchen had his hand raised to turn the spit, and the kitchen-maid had a black fowl on her lap ready to pluck.

He climbed up the stairs and saw in the hall the whole court lying asleep, and above them, on their thrones, slept the king and the queen. He continued from room to room searching for the sleeping princess. It was so quiet that he could hear his own breathing; and at last he came to the tower, went up the winding stair, and opened the door of the little room where Rosamond lay. She looked so lovely in her sleep, and he stooped and kissed her.

As she awakened she opened her eyes and smiled at him. He helped Rosamond to her feet, and they walked down the stairs to the throne room. Rosamond rushed to her parents, who were now awake, as was the rest of the court, and gave them hugs.

The horses in the yard got up and shook themselves, the hounds sprang up and wagged their tails, the pigeons on the roof drew their heads from under their wings, looked round, and flew into the field. The flies on the wall crept on a little farther. The kitchen fire leapt up and blazed and cooked the meat. The joint on the spit began to roast, as the cook cranked the spit. And the maid went on plucking the fowl.

The wedding of the Prince and Rosamond was a grand event and they lived very happily together until their lives' end.

Pleasant Ending

The king had learned a very important lesson from the grand feast he had given one hundred years before to celebrate the birth of his daughter. He made sure that everyone was invited to the wedding and there were enough golden plates for everyone to eat from.

There were no undesirable incidents at the wedding or at the feast that followed. Well, except for a few folks who imbibed a bit too much which resulted in a few ceramic vases and what-nots being broken. And although the pieces were now considered antiques- being over 100 years old and all - the king and queen felt it was a small price to pay.

Just Desserts Ending

The thirteen wise women who attended baby Rosamond's celebration were actually fairies. And so they were still very much alive and kicking during the one hundred years that had passed.

The twelfth fairy, the one who had changed the prophecy from death to sleep, had kept tabs on the beautiful Rosamond and her family. Delighted that a brave, kind prince had found Rosamond, and they were now getting married, the twelfth fairy decided it was time for the thirteenth fairy to pay for her inconsiderate "gift."

So she gathered her sister fairies, and they located the thirteenth fairy, who had been laying low these last one hundred years. They offered her a Hobson's choice, be banished from the earth forever or limit herself to bestowing only favorable "gifts" – which would have to be pre-approved by the other fairies.

Which do you think she chose?

The Princess and the Frog

There once was a Princess who often spent time alone in the palace gardens while she tossed around her favorite glowing golden ball. She didn't really like spending all her time alone, but there wasn't anyone else her age in the palace. And, if we are being honest, even if there was someone her age, they probably wouldn't have wanted to spend time with her as she was spoiled AND selfish.

Now, the problem with playing ball alone was that no one was ever there to catch the ball if she tossed it too high in the air. One day, as she was running around the flowers and hedges, she tossed her ball higher in the air than she ever had before. She was proud of her accomplishment until she heard ...

SPLASH!!

Her beautiful golden ball had plopped right into a small pond nearby! She ran over to the pond and watched sadly as the golden sphere sank deeper and deeper into the water.

She wanted her ball back desperately, but she was wearing her favorite golden dress; the gems on the front of the brilliant gown were rare and she was afraid that if she entered the water she would destroy her dress. Frustrated, the princess began to cry.

Suddenly, the Princess heard a strange noise coming from the middle of the water. *Hop, plop! Hop, plop!*

"Do you not know how to swim?" asked a small voice. The Princess looked up and scrunched her face up at the sight of a green creature sitting on the lily pad. It was a small frog.

"I do," she replied.

"Well, why don't you come on in?" he asked.

"I don't want to spoil my beautiful dress!" the Princess replied, rolling her eyes at the frog.

"Well, I suppose I could get it for you..." the frog started.

"You can? Oh! Please do! Please do!" she cried.

But before he jumped into the water, the frog turned to her and asked: "What will you give me in return for getting your golden ball?"

"Oh! You can have anything you desire!" the Princess replied, impatient to have her ball back.

"What I would like is a friend. A friend to spend time with me, to eat supper with me, to read to me, to sleep beside me, and to kiss me goodnight!" the frog said. " Yes. Anything! Anything!" the Princess cried impatiently.

And with that, the small green frog hopped into the water and retrieved the Princess' gold ball. The minute he surfaced she grabbed the ball from him and ran around giggling and tossing her beloved ball up in the air. She had completely forgotten all about the frog.

At supper, the girl was seated at the table with her father, the King. Before either of them could take a bite, there came a small knock at the door. *Knock, knock, knock.* The King got up and walked over to open it. Now I have to stop at this point and say I am surprised that the King opens his own door, usually they have servants for that. Perhaps they all had the evening off.

Hop! Hop! Hop! In came the small green frog. The King stared at the creature, as the frog said happily, "I have come to eat supper with you, Princess!" and he hopped up on the table. The Princess grabbed the frog, tossed him outside, and slammed the door closed.

Then she turned on her heel and sat down at her spot at the table once more, ignoring the suspicious look from the King.

"Who was that, Princess?" he asked her.

"Oh, no one important," she replied.

The stern look from her father caused her face to get hot as she told him what she had promised the frog because he had rescued her golden ball from the pond. "But I don't need to do all that. He's just a frog, after all." she continued.

"A promise is a promise, Princess. We must always keep our promises," the wise King said. With that the girl slowly shuffled over to the door and reluctantly opened it up. The little frog was still outside, and he hopped with her over to the table, still sore from being tossed out the door but delighted the Princess had changed her mind.

The frog ate supper with her and the King. The princess ate slowly, trying to delay the rest of the deal she had made. She was so sullen that any attempt the frog made for conversation was met with monosyllabic answers or silence. The King said very little as, understandably, he was in shock that he was sharing a meal with a talking frog. After all, wouldn't you be?

Once the meal was concluded, the frog followed the Princess into her bedroom where she opened a book and began to read to herself.

"What are you reading?" he asked, trying to peer over her shoulder to see.

"Nothing," she replied, shrugging him off.

Sadly, the frog hopped over to her bed and sat down on her pillow. Before he could get comfortable, the Princess ran over to him, picked him up, and placed him on a settee by the window.

"But your promise!" he cried. She sighed and took him back with her to bed. She read him a bedtime story and, surprisingly, the frog was quite smart and funny. She actually enjoyed his company.

When it was time to sleep, the frog asked her for his bedtime kiss. She refused, scrunching her face in a look of horror. Sadly, the frog laid down on the pillow beside her.

The Princess extinguished her bedside candle and flopped down on her side of the bed. She turned her back to the little green creature and closed her eyes tightly, hoping that sleep would come quickly. That's when she heard the sounds coming from the other side of the bed. Not the croaking sounds a frog makes, mind you. The Princess turned over and reached her hand out to the frog's face. The frog was crying.

She was hit with a wave of guilt for making the poor frog cry. She moved closer to the frog and kissed him on his, his, his cheek? Do frogs have cheeks?

WHOOOSH!!

All of a sudden, the small green frog transformed into a handsome young prince right before her eyes; she jumped off the bed in surprise. That's when he informed her that an evil witch had put a spell on him and only a kiss from a princess could return him back to his original state.

Can you imagine such a thing happening? Well, it is a fairy tale, after all.

Pleasant Ending

Well the Princess, whose name was Antoinette, was very pleased with this unexpected result. She took the Prince by the hand and led him out of her bedroom. They knocked on her father's door. He answered it, yawning, and then stared at the handsome young man standing before him. Thinking he was dreaming, he rubbed his eyes and looked again. Nope, the young man was not a hallucination.

So the King demanded, "Who are you and what are you doing in my home at this late hour?" The Prince and Princess explained that he was the frog that had rescued her golden ball from the pond.

It was an outrageous story, as I'm sure you'll agree, but eventually the King believed it. After all, witches were always casting evil spells on innocents in their day and age.

The Princess was too young to marry, but she and the Prince spent the next few years getting to know each other and eventually they did marry and live happily ever after. Although I do have to say that when the Princess became pregnant with their first child, many members of the court held their breath at the birth until they saw that the child was human and not a tadpole!

Just Desserts Ending

A true fairy tale ending, right? Tugs on your heart strings, right? But let's think this over for a moment or two.

You might remember that I mentioned early on that Antoinette is spoiled and selfish. Well, being responsible for transforming a frog into a prince did nothing to improve her disposition. She began bragging to anyone she met, "Did you know, I have the power to transform a frog into a prince?" Most people were appropriately awed, which, as you might imagine, just added fuel to the fire.

It just so happens that the word spread to a nearby kingdom where another princess, Princess Sarah, lived. Now

Princess Sarah had never met Princess Antoinette, but she was jealous of her acclaimed beauty.

Since then, she had dreamed of finding a way to take Antoinette down a notch or two and then she heard from someone in her court about Antoinette's amazing ability to transform a frog into a prince. This just might be the ticket.

Princess Sarah was used to having servants do all the tasks that required manual labor for her, but this was too important. She put on her oldest gown and her oldest slippers and went down to a nearby pond. She had borrowed a bucket from the maid and a butterfly net from the cook's grandson. She sat down on a large rock beside the pond and waited as day turned to dusk.

"Ribbit, ribbit." Ah, that was the sound she had been waiting for. She gripped the handle of the butterfly net, bent down, and readied herself. "Ribbit, ribbit," she heard again. She moved her arm up and as soon as she saw the frog she swiftly lowered her arm and caught him in the net. Sweet success!

She added some pond water to the bucket and unceremoniously dumped the startled frog into the bucket. Now for the next part of her plan.

The next morning, Princess Sarah sent a court messenger to Princess Antoinette inviting her to afternoon tea the following day. The invitation included a mysterious message that there would be a surprise guest at the tea.

Princess Antoinette was intrigued. The following day one of her father's coachmen drove her to the tea party in her personal golden carriage with rose colored velvet seats. As they rode, Antoinette kept wondering who the special guest might be. At no time did she wonder why Princess Sarah, a complete stranger to Antoinette, would have invited her in the first place. She just assumed that Sarah had heard of her great beauty and wanted to meet her in person and spend time with her.

The coach arrived after several hours of travel and the coachman assisted Princess Antoinette to disembark from the carriage. She walked up to the beautiful, ornately carved wooden doors which were immediately opened by a man servant. The servant bowed and then asked Princess Antoinette to please follow him. He led Princess Antoinette down a stunning marble hallway with walls covered in gorgeous tapestries and out a set of doors onto a beautiful stone patio.

On the patio stood a table covered with a lovely lavender tablecloth and delicate China plates and teacups. Standing next to the table in an elegant lavender gown a few hues darker than the tablecloth, stood a smiling young woman with shoulder length auburn hair. She took a few steps closer to Antoinette and reached out her hand.

Still smiling, she said, "Princess Antoinette, it's so nice to finally meet you. I am Sarah."

Princess Antoinette took her hand and said, "It's nice to meet you, too."

"Let's sit down, shall we," Sarah said motioning to the table. As Antoinette took a seat, she surreptitiously looked around for the surprise guest.

A young maid served them tea sandwiches and little cakes. Princess Sarah told her she'd pour their tea and dismissed her with a smile. Antoinette began to eat waiting for Sarah to mention the surprise guest, but Sarah said nothing about him or her. Instead she made small talk which Antoinette returned in kind.

Toward the end of their tea, Princess Sarah smiled at Antoinette and said, "You are truly beautiful."

"Thank you," replied Antoinette with a smile. So it was true that Sarah had invited her here in order to see her beauty in person.

But then Sarah threw her a curve ball. "Is it true that you can turn a frog into a prince?"

"Uh, why yes," replied Antoinette.

"Ta Da!" cried Sarah as she revealed the bucket she had hidden next to her chair. Antoinette looked confused until Sarah reached in and pulled out a frog.

"Oh," said Antoinette, "is that the special guest?"

"Yes," said Sarah. "I'd like you to turn him into a prince for me."

"I ... I don't know..." started Antoinette.

"Well I've heard that you bra... um, tell others that you have this special gift. You have your prince. I'd like to have mine."

"I have only tried it once," said Antoinette trying to determine a way out of the situation. After all, kissing a frog once had been no picnic.

"Oh come on," said Princess Sarah. "Please share your wonderful gift with me." Flattery, of course, was exactly what Antoinette needed to hear.

"Well, all right," she said. Princess Sarah held the frog close to Antoinette, Antoinette leaned in and puckered her lips trying not to think of the smell of the frog and the texture of his skin. She gave the frog a hasty kiss.

"Ribbit, ribbit, ribbit," said the male frog. "Ribbit, ribbit, ribbit," answered the female frog formerly known as Princess Antoinette. The two frogs hopped off together. Did they live happily ever after together? I have no idea.

But I can tell you that once the Prince, formerly known as the Frog Prince, who had married Princess Antoinette, got over his broken heart he began courting Princess Sarah. Did they live happily ever after together? I'll leave that to you to decide.

Rapunzel

O nce upon a time, a young, married couple waited for the birth of their first child. They lived in a little house near a garden in which all sorts of fruit and vegetables grew. The woman often looked at their neighbor's garden through the window and developed a craving for the rampion that grew in abundance. Her husband offered her other foods, but she insisted that rampion was the only thing she wanted to eat. And its hard to argue with a pregnant woman who is having cravings.

But, since the owner of the garden was an evil Witch, her husband didn't dare ask her for some of the rampion, so he decided to steal some. Foolish man, right? After all, she was a witch. So as soon as he stepped into the garden he heard a noise. The Witch yelled at him and asked him how he dares to steal from her garden. He fell down on his knees and asked her to spare him because he just wanted some rampions for his wife.

The Witch was so evil that she told him he will get the rampion only if he gives her his firstborn child or she will turn him into a pig. The husband felt he didn't have a choice, so he agreed.

After a few months, the woman gave birth to a little girl, and the Witch took her away. She named her Rapunzel. Time passed and Rapunzel became a beautiful young woman with long blonde hair. I don't know if it was due to her mother eating so many rampions, but her hair grew very, very long.

The Witch locked Rapunzel away in an isolated tower that had no stairs. I'm sure you are wondering how the Witch visited her if there were no stairs. Well, that's where her long hair came in. The Witch visited Rapunzel every day and would call to let down her hair, and then the Witch would climb up that long, long hair.

Rapunzel never saw anyone except the witch, who she thought was her mother. There was only a small window on the top of the tower at which the beautiful girl would often sit and stare out at the outside world and sing lovely songs. One day a Prince, who was passing through the woods, heard her. He hid in the bushes nearby and enjoyed her singing until the Witch arrived and called to her to let down her hair.

Once the witch left the prince called Rapunzel to let her hair down. Rapunzel wondered why her mother had returned so soon, but she let her hair down. The Prince climbed to her room, and when Rapunzel saw him, she got scared.

But the Prince had a disarming smile and he spoke quietly to her. When he learned she had spent all her life in that tower, he told her about the outside world. She enjoyed his stories and began to fall in love with him.

With Rapunzel's permission, the Prince began to visit her daily, but she cautioned him that his visits needed to be kept secret as Rapunzel was not sure how "her mother" would react. The Prince agreed and soon he also fell in love with her.

The Witch still came to see Rapunzel every day but was unaware that Rapunzel had another daily visitor. One morning Rapunzel accidentally said that she was harder to pull up than the Prince. Immediately, after uttering this, Rapunzel knew it had been a mistake.

The Witch was furious, and she started yelling at Rapunzel. She told her she was an ungrateful brat and reprimanded her. The Witch grabbed Rapunzel by the hair and cut it off. With her long hair lying on the floor, Rapunzel was sentenced to a lifetime of loneliness and misery in the tower.

The Witch waited until the Prince came and called for Rapunzel to let her hair down and then she threw the cut-off hair out the window and held on to the other end. He started climbing. When he reached the window, the Witch grinned her evil grin and let go of the hair. He fell into the thorny bushes below and became blind.

The Witch then muttered an incantation and sent the Prince faraway. He searched for his Rapunzel from city to city, village to village but she was nowhere to be found. He fed on berries and drank the water from the rivers. His misery was growing by the day as he pictured his beautiful Rapunzel and her voice.

He wandered for years when he came to a forest where he sat under a tree and cried. He was about to give up his search when he heard a well-known voice. It was his Rapunzel. The Witch had moved Rapunzel out of the tower and into a little cottage deep, deep into the same forest that the Prince had stumbled upon.

He gathered the last bits of his strength and moved towards that beautiful voice. He held on to the trees, stumbled and got stuck in the bushes while he was calling for his Rapunzel.

Rapunzel heard his call. She started running toward the sound of his voice. Finally she spotted him and ran to his arms. It was true love. Rapunzel started crying, and her tears healed his eyes.

They went to his castle where they got married. They loved each other and lived happily ever after.

Pleasant Ending

The story already has a pleasant ending but wait, there's more. Rapunzel became pregnant with their first child. And, no, she did not crave rampion during her pregnancy – in case that's where your mind was going.

The Prince's parents were so excited to be grandparents for the first time. Rapunzel was glad they were so happy, but she wished that their child could have both sets of grandparents in his or her life.

So, Rapunzel asked her husband, Prince Richard, if he could search for her real parents. Now remember this was back in the days before records were kept of births or deaths so this was a tall order. Prince Richard told his wife that this would be difficult to accomplish, but she asked him over and over again. Remember what I said at the beginning of the story about dealing with a pregnant woman? Finally, Prince Richard told his wife, who he loved dearly, that he would try his best to find her parents.

Now Prince Richard had no idea of how to go about such a seemingly impossible task. Since his wife left her parents as a baby, she had no recollection of where she was born or what their names were. But Prince Richard was an intelligent man who knew you sometimes needed to ask others for help. He went to his mother for advice.

And that's when Prince Richard learned something about his mother that she had kept hidden from everyone except his father. You see, before she had caught the eye of Richard's father, she had been a gypsy with the ability to see the future as well as the past. Now she had not used any of her unique skills since she had married, but she got out her crystal ball and after a few minutes she was able to locate Rapunzel's parents. They were living in the same small cottage where Rapunzel had been born.

Prince Richard kissed his mother's cheek, thanked her, and headed as quickly as he could on his favorite mount to the little house. He took with him the little bracelet that Rapunzel had worn as a babe on her wrist and now wore on a chain around her neck as proof of who she was. Rapunzel had given him the bracelet when he had agreed to try to find her parents, but she had no idea that he was on his way to her birthplace.

His journey took several days, and Prince Richard arrived a bit disheveled and very tired. He knocked on the door and it was opened by Rapunzel's mother. He knew it was her mother because she looked like an older version of his beloved.

Prince Richard explained that he was the husband of the woman he believed to have been born in this house and he held up the little bracelet. Rapunzel's mother gasped, shook her head yes and called for her husband. The couple could not believe that their daughter was alive and doing well. And, they were going to become grandparents!

In a matter of a few days, there was a grand reunion at the castle. A celebration like no other! And Rapunzel was the happiest princess in the world!

Just Desserts Ending

Of course we haven't mentioned the antagonist of the original story – the evil Witch. Just what happened to her?

Well, when the Witch returned from whatever she was doing the day Rapunzel heard her true love calling for her and saw that Rapunzel was gone she flew into a rage. Now with all of her powers, the Witch probably could have found Rapunzel and Prince Richard easily but the rage she felt was grander than any other rage she had ever experienced.

She screamed until her face turned crimson. She stamped her feet on the earthen floor of the little cottage until one foot actually sunk into the dirt. This, of course, just enraged her more. She screeched even louder, scaring all of the forest animals and birds into hiding. Her arms were flailing as she tried to remove her foot from the ground. Her shrieking grew louder and louder until her voice was silenced.

There were no sounds coming from the little cottage. A few brave forest animals returned and one, I believe it was a courageous raccoon, looked in the window. The evil Witch was lying motionless on the floor.

"Ding, dong the witch is dead. The evil witch is dead."

If a doctor had been on hand, he probably would have pronounced that the Witch had had a heart attack. But, there was no doctor nearby and no one to summon one so I guess we will never know for sure.

King Thrushbeard

There was once a King who had a daughter who was beautiful beyond all measure, but she was so proud and haughty that no suitor was good enough for her. She sent away one after the other and ridiculed them as well.

Once the King had a great feast and invited all the young men eligible to marry. They came from near and far. The King's daughter was led through the ranks, but to every one of them she had some objection to make; one was too fat. Another was too tall. The third was too short. The fourth was too pale. The fifth was too red. And so on. But she made herself especially merry over a good king whose chin had grown a little crooked.

"Well," she cried and laughed, "he has a chin like a thrush's beak!" and from that time he got the name of King Thrushbeard.

Her father was very angry at the way she mocked her suitors and swore that the very first beggar that came to his doors would be her husband.

A few days afterwards a fiddler came and sang beneath the windows, trying to earn some coin. When the King heard him he said, "Let him come up." So the fiddler came in, in his dirty, ragged clothes, and sang before the King and his daughter, and when he had ended he asked for a trifling gift. The King said, "Your song has pleased me so well that I will give you my daughter as your wife."

The King's daughter shuddered, but the King said, "I have taken an oath to give you to the very first beggar and I will keep it." Anything she said was in vain; the priest was brought, and she was wedded to the fiddler on the spot. When that was done the King said, "Now it is not proper for you, a beggar-woman, to stay any longer in my palace, you may just go away with your husband."

Her new husband led her out by the hand, and she was obliged to walk away on foot with him. When they came to a large forest she asked, "To whom does that beautiful forest belong?"

"It belongs to King Thrushbeard; if you had taken him, it would have been yours."

Afterwards they came to a meadow, and she asked again, "To whom does this beautiful green meadow belong?"

"It belongs to King Thrushbeard; if you had taken him, it would have been yours."

Then they came to a large town, and she asked again, "To whom does this fine large town belong?"

"It belongs to King Thrushbeard; if you had taken him, it would have been yours."

"It does not please me," said the fiddler, "to hear you always wishing for another husband; am I not good enough for you?"

At last they came to a very little hut, and she said, "Oh goodness! What a small house; to whom does this miserable, little hovel belong?"

The fiddler answered, "That is my house and yours, where we shall live together."

She had to stoop in order to go in at the low door. "Where are the servants?" asked the King's daughter.

"What servants?" answered her husband. "You must do things for yourself. Make a fire at once, and set on water to cook my supper, for I am quite tired." But the King's daughter knew nothing about lighting fires or cooking, and her husband had to show her how to do everything.

When they had finished their scanty meal they went to bed. He woke her up quite early in the morning in order to take care of the household chores.

For a few days they lived in this way, but their provisions were growing low so her husband told her she must weave baskets to sell. He went out, cut some willows, and brought them home. Then she began to weave, but the tough willows wounded her delicate hands.

"I see that this will not do," said the man. "You had better spin, perhaps you can do that better." She sat down and tried to spin, but the hard thread soon cut her soft fingers and made them bleed. " Humph," said her husband. "It seems you are fit for no sort of work. I have made a bad bargain with you. Perhaps you'll do better at sales. You will take these pots and earthenware to the marketplace and sell them.

On her first day, she succeeded well, for the people were glad to buy the woman's wares because she was good-looking. They paid her what she asked and many even gave her the money and left the pots with her as well. So they lived on what she had earned as long as it lasted, then the husband bought a lot of new crockery. With this she sat down at the corner of the marketplace and set it out ready for sale. But suddenly there came a drunken man galloping along, and he rode right amongst the pots so that they were all broken into a thousand bits. She began to weep, unsure of how her husband would react.

She ran home and told him of the misfortune.

"Who would seat herself at a corner of the marketplace with crockery?" said the man. "I see very well that you cannot do any ordinary work, so I have been to our King's palace and have asked whether they cannot find a place for a kitchen-maid, and they have promised me to take you, so you'll get your food for nothing."

The King's daughter was now a kitchen maid and had to be at the cook's beck and call and do the dirtiest work. In both her pockets she fastened a little jar, in which she took home her share of the leftovers and upon this they lived.

It happened that the wedding of the King's eldest son was to be celebrated, and she placed herself by the door of the hall to look on. As she watched the festivities, she cursed the pride and haughtiness which had humbled her and brought her to so great poverty.

The smell of the delicious dishes which were being taken in and out reached her, and now and then the servants threw her a few morsels of them which she put in her jars to take home.

All at once the King's son entered, clothed in velvet and silk, with gold chains about his neck. And when he saw the beautiful woman standing by the door he seized her by the hand and would have danced with her. But she refused and shrank with fear, for she saw that it was King Thrushbeard, the suitor whom she had mocked.

Her struggles were of no avail as he drew her into the hall; but the string by which her pockets were hung broke. The jars fell out, broke, and the scraps of food were scattered all about.

When the people saw it, they began to laugh, and she was so ashamed that she wanted to sink into the ground. She sprang to the door and would have run away, but on the stairs a man caught her and brought her back; and when she looked at him it was King Thrushbeard again.

He said to her kindly, "Do not be afraid, my dear one. Don't you recognize me? I am your husband, the fiddler. I was also the ruffian who rode through your crockery. This was all done to humble your proud spirit, and to punish you for the insolence with which you mocked me."

She wept bitterly and said, "I have done great wrong, and am not worthy to be your wife."

But he said, "I think you have changed. Now, let's celebrate our wedding." Then the maids-in-waiting came and dressed her in the most splendid clothing, and her father and his whole court came and wished her happiness in her marriage with King Thrushbeard. And the joy now began in earnest.

Pleasant Ending

The new Queen, whose name was Elizabeth, had learned her lesson well.

Several times a year she insisted that they open the castle and its grounds to all the people. She would organize grand feasts with music and dancing. The people of the kingdom grew to love their Queen.

Over the years she taught all of their children to respect everyone from the scullery maids to the guards and everyone in between. She was always reminding their children that even though they were princes and princesses, their servants deserved politeness and courtesy.

Queen Elizabeth would take her children for strolls through the village and greet many of the people by name or take a few moments to pass the time of day. She was truly a changed woman and all thanks to her husband, King Thrushbeard.

Just Desserts Ending

The new Queen, whose name was Elizabeth, had learned her lesson well.

Over the years she spent time teaching and reminding their children to be polite to all of their servants. Most of them listened to her and treated the servants with respect, but there were times...

One of their daughters, Raven, was a bit of an imp. She was constantly playing tricks on various members of staff. She put a snake, a harmless garter snake, but a snake, in her bed one morning. The maid came into her bedroom to dust and change her linens but hurriedly left Raven's room screaming!

Queen Elizabeth was quite upset with Raven, as you might imagine. Raven was sent to her room without her afternoon tea. But she did not care. This just gave her the opportunity to plan her next escapade. Besides, she had some sweets hidden in her room, so she did not go hungry.

The next day, Raven was ready. She went out to the castle's pond and grabbed what she needed to execute her plan. This time she waited until the family had afternoon tea and the cooks and scullery maids had sufficient time to wash their tea things.

Raven knew that after that, the kitchen staff would go into the small room off the kitchen to have their tea. That's when Raven slipped into the kitchen. She put her pond dweller into the crock that held the flour. Then she went outside to play with her siblings.

That evening, about an hour before dinner was to be served, there were blood curdling screams from the kitchen. King Thrushbeard rushed in to find the cook and the cook's assistant on top of the preparation tables. Puzzled, he looked around and saw a white something hopping around the kitchen. "Raven!" he shouted through clenched teeth.

He caught the flour-covered frog and helped the cook and her assistant down from the table. Apologizing profusely, he promised it would not happen again. He also told them that Raven would be punished for her actions. Raven was sent, once again, to her room but there was more to come. Her mother and father discussed the best punishment for her actions.

The next day, Raven found that all of her beautiful gowns were missing from her closet. In their place were several plain, rough gowns. Puzzled, Raven put one of the gowns on and went down to breakfast. When she entered the dining room she discovered that it had not yet been served.

One of the scullery maids came into the dining room and said a bit roughly, "Well there you are lazy bones. Get into the kitchen and give us a hand." Still befuddled, Raven followed her into the kitchen.

The cook looked at her and ordered, "You can start by sweeping the floor near the fireplace."

"Me, sweep?" asked Raven.

"Yes, you sweep. Haven't you spoken to your parents yet?"

"No," Raven replied.

"Ah," the cook said. "I expect they are having a bit of a lie in. I'm sure they will talk to you later. Now grab that broom."

Raven spent the rest of the morning working in the kitchen. When she asked about breakfast, all of the kitchen staff laughed. One of the younger scullery maids, feeling a little bit sorry for the Princess, said, "We eat after the King and Queen and the family eat." Eventually breakfast was served to the royal family and the clean up was completed. That's when Raven finally got something to eat.

After she had eaten, she was summoned to her parents. Her mother said, "Raven, we have been very disappointed in your actions. We've tried talking to you and taking away some privileges, but none of that has worked."

Then her father spoke, "So we have decided that you need to experience the arduous work that is done by others so that our lives are easier. You will work in the kitchen in the mornings, and you will help the maids dust and clean in the afternoons. The evenings will be free for you to spend in your room to relax or play games with your siblings."

Raven looked in disbelief at her parents. But she did not question what they had said for she could see in their eyes that they were serious. The only thing she asked with a lump in her throat was, "For how long?"

Her mother's response was quick, "For as long as it takes."

It was a hard lesson, but after a few weeks Raven grew to respect the staff and the work they did. Her parents felt it too and so she was able to return to her life as a member of the royal family, a princess.

Did she continue her good behavior? Well, she was her mother's daughter after all, so I think the chances are good that she did.

The Twelve Dancing Princesses

There was once a King who had twelve daughters, each one more beautiful than the other. They all slept together in one chamber, with their beds standing side by side. Every night when they were in their beds, the King locked the door and bolted it. But in the morning when he unlocked the door, he saw that their shoes were worn out as if they had been dancing all night. No one could determine how this had happened. And, of course, his daughters would not confess to leaving their room.

The King was so desperate to find out what was happening, that he issued a proclamation that any man who could discover where they went at night, could choose one of them for his wife and be King after his death. But as so often happens with these proclamations, there was a catch. If the discovery was not made within three days and nights the man would have to forfeit his life. This, of course, was often done to insure that only brave and dedicated men would apply.

Not long after the proclamation, a King's son presented himself, and offered to undertake the enterprise. He was led into a room adjoining the princesses' sleeping chamber. His bed was placed there, and the door of their room was left open. But the eyelids of the prince grew heavy, and he fell asleep, and when he awoke in the morning, he knew that all twelve had been out of their room for their shoes had holes in the soles.

On the second and third nights everything occurred just the same, and so the young prince lost his head. Many others came after this and undertook the enterprise, but all forfeited their lives.

After a time a poor soldier, who had been wounded, found himself on the road to the town where the King lived. There he met an old woman, who asked him where he was going.

"I have no idea," he answered. And then he added in jest, "I have half a mind to discover where the princesses go and dance their shoes into holes, and thus become King."

"That is not so difficult," said the old woman, "you must not drink the wine which will be brought to you at night and must pretend to be sound asleep." With that she gave him a cloak, and said, "If you put on that, you will be invisible, and then you can follow the twelve princesses unseen." The soldier thanked the old woman for her advice, and the cloak, and made his way to the King where he announced himself as a suitor.

He was well received and given royal garments to wear. That evening at bedtime he was taken to the antechamber, and as he was about to go to bed, the eldest princess came and brought him a cup of wine. He averted her attention and poured the wine into a nearby planter. Then he feigned extreme tiredness and told the princess he must lay down. After a while, he began to snore, as if in the deepest sleep.

The twelve princesses heard that and laughed. They got up, opened wardrobes and cupboards, and brought out pretty dresses and slippers. Once dressed they began to leave, but the youngest said, "I have the strangest feeling that some misfortune is about to befall us."

The eldest sister replied, "You are being a silly goose. He is fast asleep like the others." They all looked at the soldier, but his eyes were closed, and he did not move or stir, so they felt quite safe.

The eldest then went to her bed and tapped it. It immediately sank into the earth, and one after the other they descended through the opening, the eldest going first. The soldier, who had watched everything, put on his cloak, and went down last following the youngest. Halfway down the stairs he trod a little on her gown.

She cried out, "What is that? Who is pulling my dress?"

"Don't be so silly!" said the eldest, "You have caught it on a nail."

When they reached the bottom of the stairs, they were standing in a wonderfully pretty avenue of trees, with leaves of silver, that shone and glistened. The soldier thought, "I must take away a token," and he broke off a twig from one of the trees. The tree cracked loudly.

The youngest cried out again. "Something is wrong, did you hear the crack?"

But the eldest said, "It is a gun fired for joy, because we have gotten rid of our prince so quickly."

Next they came to an avenue where all the leaves were of gold, and lastly into a third where they were of bright diamonds. He broke off a twig from each, which made such a crack each time that the youngest cried out, but the eldest still maintained that they were salutes.

They went on and came to a great lake whereon stood twelve little boats, and in every boat sat a handsome prince, all of whom were waiting for the twelve princesses. Each prince took one of them with him, but the soldier seated himself by the youngest.

Her prince said, "I can't tell why the boat is so much heavier today. I shall have to row with all my strength if I am to get it across."

On the opposite side of the lake stood a splendid, brightly lit castle, which vibrated from the joyous music of trumpets and kettledrums. They rowed over there, entered, and each prince danced with the girl he loved. The soldier danced with them unseen, and when one of them had a cup of wine in her hand he drank it up, so that the cup was empty when she carried it to her mouth. The youngest was alarmed at this, but the eldest always made her be silent.

They danced there until three o'clock in the morning when all the shoes were danced into holes, and they were forced to leave. The princes rowed them back again over the lake, and this time the soldier seated himself by the eldest. On the shore they took leave of their princes and promised to return the following night. When they reached the stairs the soldier ran on ahead and lay down in his bed. The twelve had come up slowly and wearily and they heard the soldier snoring loudly.

They said, "So far as he is concerned, we are safe."

They took off their beautiful dresses and put them away. Then they placed their worn-out shoes under the bed.

The next day, the soldier said nothing about what he had seen. That night he faked drinking the wine again and then followed the princesses under his cloak. Everything happened just as it had the first night.

The third night was just the same, except the soldier took one of the goblets away with him as a token. When the hour had arrived for him to give his answer, he took the three twigs and the goblet, and went to the King. The twelve princesses stood behind the door, and listened to what he was going to say.

When the King asked, "Where have my twelve daughters gone to dance their shoes to pieces in the night?"

The soldier answered, "In an underground castle with twelve princes." Then he related how it had come to pass and brought out the tokens. The King then summoned his daughters and asked them if the soldier had told the truth, and when they saw that they were betrayed, they were obliged to confess all. Thereupon the King asked which of them he would have for his wife?

He answered, "I am no longer young, so give me the eldest."

The wedding was celebrated on the same day, and the kingdom was promised to him after the King's death.

And the twelve princes from that underground king-dom? They were bewitched for as many days as they had danced nights with the twelve princesses.

Pleasant Ending

Well, the original ending is already pleasant enough for the soldier, and hopefully for the eldest princess as well. But what of her eleven sisters?

Well, the King made sure that the staircase to the underground kingdom was filled with rocks and the opening sealed off. He also moved their bed chamber to another part of the castle. This, of course, was to ensure there were no more nightly dancing excursions.

The King, however, had a soft spot for his daughters and, with the help of his eldest daughter, began to arrange weekly balls at his castle. This would give them the opportunity to dance but under the watchful eye of their father, as well as the chance to meet young, eligible men.

Of course the King had never met the princes from the underground kingdom, so he did not realize that they had found another way to his castle – once their bewitching had worn off – and began to appear at the balls to dance with his daughters. Each of the young princes spent time talking to the King about subjects that the princesses had informed them that their father enjoyed. The King was quite taken by these polite young men, and after a time, gave permission for them to marry his daughters.

A grand wedding ceremony was planned, one like no one had ever seen before, and twelve princesses were married to the twelve princes from the underground kingdom. The castle was exquisitely decorated, the food served at the wedding reception was delicious and fireworks were set off at the end of the evening.

But, if you've been keeping count, you might be wondering who the eldest prince married since his "girl" had already married the soldier. Well, he had met one of the King's nieces at the weekly balls and she was also a princess. So twelve princesses married twelve princes. And hopefully they all lived happily ever after.

Just Desserts Ending

When the twelve princes awoke from their bewitchment they were miffed, to say the least. After all, they felt they had been blameless and yet they had endured a punishment from the King. They decided to exact some justice, or maybe some revenge.

Then they heard about the weekly balls that the princesses' father was conducting. They put their heads together and came up with a plan.

Although the King had sealed his daughters' entrance to their kingdom, the princes had other ways to leave their underground world. On the night of one of the balls, they put on their finest clothing and rode in golden coaches to the castle.

They entered the castle and quickly located their lovely ladies and began to dance with them. The eleven sisters were delighted to see their princes again. Their young men whispered in their ears and told them of the plan for the evening.

Now the eldest prince had trouble finding his beloved for a while and then he found her by the side of her husband. He asked if she was happy, and she replied that she was. She could see the disappointment on his face and offered to introduce him to her cousin, a lovely young lady who was also a princess and an expert dancer.

He danced with this beauty and asked her if she had ever dreamed of an adventure. She replied that her life was very dull and every night she dreamed of adventures.

Encouraged by this, the eldest prince whispered the plan for the evening. She smiled and agreed.

One by one, over a period of several hours, each prince danced his princess out the back garden doors where the coachmen had placed the golden coaches. And, one by one, each coach left the ball with one prince and one princess inside.

They arrived at the magical entrance to the underground kingdom where a priest stood to marry each couple. Then each newlywed couple descended the golden staircase to the kingdom below.

In the meantime, back at the ball, the King had noticed that eleven of his daughters were no longer on the dance floor. He asked his eldest daughter and her husband if they had seen them. That's when she noticed her cousin was also missing.

A search of the grounds was made, but the princesses were nowhere to be found. The eldest sister started sobbing and became hysterical. She finally confessed to her father that the twelve princes had been at the ball, and she had introduced her cousin to the eldest. At the time she had seen no harm in any of this.

The King became furious. He demanded that his daughter tell him the location of the other entrance to their kingdom, but she did not know where it was for she and her sisters had always used the one he had sealed. He took one look at his traumatized daughter and knew she was telling the truth.

There was only one thing to do. King ordered some of his guards to follow him to the princesses' original bed-chamber. They moved the bed that had been covering the opening prepared to unseal it. But the opening was gone – it had vanished.

For the next few years, the King and his men searched and searched for the entrance to the underground kingdom, but it was never found. For the rest of his days the King regretted that he had those twelve princes bewitched and had interfered with the love lives of his daughters for he never saw his daughters again.

About the author

Teri Lott taught elementary school for thirty years. When she retired she thought, what's next? Well, she turned her gift for gab and love of stories (she's never without a book) into a second career and became a professional storyteller.

In 2020, Teri wrote her first book filled with original and reimagined stories– *Lots of Tales: Stories that Grow your Children*. Since then she has published other books for children and their families.

Teri has always loved hearing and telling fairy tales. The idea for this book has been bouncing around in her brain for several years. And now, it is finally a book!

Teri enjoys spending time with her friends and family and likes to go shopping, especially for puppets! She lives in southeastern Ohio on five acres with her hubby.

Also by

Other books by Teri:
Lots of Tales: Stories that Grow with Your Children
Lots of Tales, Too: Seasonal Stories that Grow with Your Children
Jackie Tales, The Untold Stories of Jack's Sister
* Lots of Animal Tales*

You can find Teri's books on Amazon or contact her at lotts.of.tales@gmail.com.
Or, if you live in Ohio, her books are at The Ohio Art Market in Westerville, Ohio; Kicks Mix Bookstore in Newark, Ohio; Beanbag Books in Delaware, Ohio; and Grammercy Books in Bexley, Ohio.

We'd love to hear from you!

If you enjoyed this book, please leave a review on Amazon, Goodreads, or any other place you review books. Reviews not only help other readers find books they'd be interested in, but also provides feedback to the author.

You can find Teri Lott on Facebook or enjoy her multigenerational stories on YouTube (@terilott2104).

Teri's email: lotts.of.tales@gmail.com

Currently Teri is working on a sequel to Lots of Animal Tales.

Made in the USA
Middletown, DE
31 July 2024

58180815R40104